I0597593

FAILED LED PROTOCOL

CINDY BONDS

Scrivenings PRESS
Quench your thirst for story.
www.ScriveningsPress.com

Copyright © 2025 by Cindy Bonds

Published by Scrivenings Press LLC
15 Lucky Lane
Morrilton, Arkansas 72110
https://ScriveningsPress.com

Printed in the United States of America

All rights reserved. No part of this publication may be reproduced, stored in a retrieval system, or transmitted in any form or by any means—for example, electronic, photocopy and recording— without the prior written permission of the publisher. The only exception is brief quotations in printed reviews.

Paperback ISBN 978-1-64917-458-1

eBook ISBN 978-1-64917-459-8

Editors: Suzie Waltner and K. Banks

Cover design by Linda Fulkerson - www.bookmarketinggraphics.com

All characters are fictional, and any resemblance to real people, either factual or historical, is purely coincidental.

NO AI TRAINING: Without in any way limiting the author's [and publisher's] exclusive rights under copyright, any use of this publication to "train" generative artificial intelligence (AI) technologies to generate text is expressly prohibited. The author reserves all rights to license uses of this work for generative AI training and development of machine learning language models.

Thank you, Jesus, for giving me a restless mind that can write things for You and Your glory!

PROLOGUE

Grabbing the bleeding man's collar, Lance Corporal Kenton Matthews yanked him from the chair and carried his limp body through the door and down the hallway.

"We can't make it," the man slung over his shoulder muttered.

Kenton ducked into a room, shutting the door and surveilling the broom closet's materials. Shoving the man into a large trash bin, he slipped on the janitor's suit and pulled a hat down over his face.

"Keep quiet," he whispered, pressing the lid on the container.

Stepping out of the closet, he tipped the canister and rolled it behind him, several trash bags in hand. Turning the corner, he paused as a few men rushed by.

After winding his way around the corridors, he entered the loading bay. His team would be waiting just outside the fence, past the trees.

But before he could get the package to safety, two armed guards approached, yelling about being on the loading dock.

"Just doing my job," he said in Arabic, keeping his head down.

A hand seized his arm. In one move, Kenton put one man on the ground and gripped the other's throat. With both silenced, he pulled the package from the trash barrel and carried him down the dock, past the lights of the bay, and into the night.

A siren pierced the evening air. At least they were out of the building.

"I ... I can run."

"No. Quiet," he mumbled.

The man might be able to move, but keeping up would be impossible after what he'd been through.

The rushing of water guided his steps as he sprinted from the small encampment much too close to Turkey's Georgian border. Pausing at a grove of trees, he sat the man down and studied his injuries. Most were superficial, but the gaping wound in his chest still bled. The dogs would find them quickly.

Packing the chest wound with everything in his kit, Kenton wrapped his belt around the man's middle to keep it all in place. Barking echoed in the distance. Taking out the sulfur powder from his belt, he poured it around the area.

With a deep breath, he lifted the man back on his shoulder and rushed upstream. The rest of the team would be waiting.

An explosion rocked the ground as fire erupted into the night sky, highlighting the desert land.

"No." He fell to a knee.

"Just go. Leave me here."

"Shut up," he ordered, pushing to stand and changing direction.

Secondary exfil it is.

Nearing the shore of the small inlet that would lead to the Black Sea, gunfire ripped through the trees and bushes.

"Put me down and go!" The man's raspy voice mumbled from his back.

Stepping into the water, he grabbed the man in a safety hold and jumped in. The frigid current carried them downstream, still a better option than the gunfire or the dogs that got past the sulfur.

Bobbing up and down, he kept the man afloat. As they neared the trail to the exfil, Kenton pulled to the side, his body shivering and quaking.

He checked the silent man, afraid he had succumbed to the cold. Finding a steady heartbeat, Kenton pulled him back onto his shoulder, carrying him up and over the embankment. A light banished the darkness, and he dropped, covering the man and pulling his weapon.

"We know you've made it, sir. Might as well come out now." The all-too-familiar Turkish accent-laced words made his temper rage.

"Halil Rashid is behind this?" he hissed.

It couldn't be. Not this time.

"I have already disbursed your comrades, as I'm sure you know by now. I was expecting you. Come out, or the dogs will find you."

Mind racing, the only thing Kenton could think to do was return to the water. As the light swept away, he pulled the man up, carefully dragging him back to the river. Slipping in quietly, the sound of gunfire exploded, and he dove in.

The fast current bumped and rolled over rapids. Kenton pushed off and dodged as much debris and rock as possible.

Once the river narrowed, he pulled the man to the shore once again. An entry to an old tunnel opened from under the brush into the side of a mound. Lying on his belly, Kenton pulled the man in, his breathing waning. Hypothermia.

"Great, just great." Kenton pulled the man farther into the

tunnel, turning and twisting through the system, trying to find a safe place to hide.

The aged tunnel system consisted of dirt walls and crumbling ceilings from the barrage of weapons that had racked the land. These were older than any tunnels he'd yet seen. Forgotten hiding spots from wars long ago.

Lying the man on a makeshift bed in the dirt, Kenton worked to warm him with nothing but the leaves and grass that accumulated within the hole.

Car engines above them made him still.

"Find them, now!" Rashid's voice bellowed, and Kenton gritted his teeth.

Once Rashid let the dogs loose, they would be found, and something worse than death would await.

The injured man groaned.

"Quiet," Kenton whispered.

"The ... the guard."

"What?"

"The guard is us."

"Which one?"

The man's words could be ramblings from the cold, but at this point, there were no other options.

"Red ... red scarf."

Kenton pulled a knife from his boot and pushed it into the man's hands. "Just in case."

He slid on his belly through the system, cold air leading him to a small hole. He searched the darkness. Twelve heads stood out from the lights. In the dark, it was impossible to tell if any had a scarf, much less a red one.

Drifting slowly back to their hiding spot, he found the man leaning back, rubbing his arms and legs.

"Can't see. Too dark," Kenton whispered.

The man nodded. Stripping off the janitorial coverall,

Kenton wadded it up and pushed it against the man's blood-stained chest, hoping to keep the wound from seeping.

Mortars exploded farther south, shattering the silence. The tunnels wouldn't hide them long. As soon as the sun came up, the missed areas would be discovered.

Someone had to have tipped off Rashid. Otherwise, Kenton's team would be loading them up, and they'd be across the border by now. How were they found so quickly?

"Codeword, Mason," the man's hoarse voice cracked.

Kenton nodded. The problem was getting to use that word would mean capture, and by then, it would be useless.

Digging at the piled dirt, Kenton pushed through to an adjoining tunnel, searching for a better exit. Coming to a dead end, he slid on his belly back to the man.

A sudden impact from above sent pain surging through his hip and leg. He gritted his teeth, forcing himself to keep from screaming.

"You've hit a hole. Move it back." The Arabic words echoed in the night air.

The tunnel had collapsed from the weight of the vehicle above, trapping his leg. His hip seared in pain as dirt held him in place. Turning as much as he could, he hit and pushed at the dirt and rock. Grunting at the pressure, he heaved a sigh as the dirt shifted enough for him to roll out.

Taking long, deep breaths, Kenton ignored the black spots dotting his vision as he slid on his belly back to the man.

"What happened?" The man shuddered through chattering teeth.

Kenton collapsed prone, breathing into the dirt as bile burned his throat. Feeling around his hip, he felt a puncture wound seeping blood. "It's cut."

. . .

"LET ME SEE." The man's British-laced words echoed in the tunnel as hands searched the area.

Ripping his outer shirt, he handed it over.

"This is going to hurt."

Grabbing a root from the ground, Kenton pulled it up and shoved it between his teeth just before a blinding pain made his body go limp as he passed out.

WAKING WITH A START, Kenton searched the area, groaning to find himself still in the hole, still hurting and still trapped.

"You're alive." The whispered voice shuddered. He turned, surprised to see the Brit still awake.

"Didn't think you'd be." Kenton forced himself to sit up, wincing at the burn through his hip.

"You're lucky it was a small wound," whispered his fellow spy.

Pushing into the small crevice with the man, he leaned back against the rock and exhaled heavily.

"We should pray."

Kenton looked over the ragged man. Although he didn't have the man's name, he knew he was important. Important enough for his government to intervene while in-country on other matters. "No point."

"No?"

Kenton shook his head, breathing through his mouth and trying to slow down before he hyperventilated.

"God is more real than you know."

He chuckled low. "Sure, an all-powerful God that allows the kind of evil in this world we've seen." He sighed. "We're dead either way, man."

The man just shook his head with a raised eyebrow. "Not me. Perhaps you."

He chuckled again.

"Marcus Moore. And you are?"

Normally, giving out names wasn't part of the deal. But then again, since they were about to die …

"Kenton Matthews. Why didn't your government intervene?"

Moore frowned.

"Tats are always a bad idea." He nodded to where the man's chest had been opened. "I saw the ink when I was packing the wound. Doesn't SAS take care of their own?"

Moore sighed. "Already tried. You must have caught him off guard."

He smiled. "That's how Army Recon does things." He winked and laid his head back.

"We get out of this, Kenton, I have something to share with you about God."

"We get out of this, I might just believe it was a miracle."

Another mortar hit, farther away.

"They're looking closer to the river. We might have a chance if I could run."

The moonlight edged in through the various holes around them. Something sticking up from the tunnel caught his eye.

"Was that there before I passed out?" Kenton glanced at Moore, who turned to look and then shook his head. Pulling himself on his belly across the tunnel, he snatched it from the light and brought it back for Moore to see.

"Our man." Moore fingered the tattered red fabric. "He must've heard us or seen the opening we came through."

Grabbing Moore's arm, Kenton indicated for him to follow, crawling back through the tunnel to the small opening. Slowly pushing at the dirt, he pulled and prodded to make a larger hole. He could now see a few men facing the water. The brake lights of a truck started for their location, and he ducked down. Men's voices became audible.

"Get that truck away. The ground isn't sturdy. One already fell through."

"Yes, sir."

This was their only chance.

Heaving Moore to his feet, Kenton pushed him through the hole, then followed. In one move, he tossed Moore into the truck and jumped in the back as well, sinking as low as possible as the engine revved.

After a few minutes, the truck suddenly stopped. Footsteps neared and then departed as the weight of two duffle bags landed on top of them. Kenton cut into the nearest bag and pulled out a uniform similar to the assailants'. Wriggling into it was sheer pain.

He paused at the sound of a vehicle approaching, hat halfway to his head. From behind the bags, he could just see a box truck pull in front of them.

He slid from the back and into the driver's seat, securing the hat firmly in place and cranking the engine to follow the truck down the road. Gritting his teeth, he slowed, hoping to give Moore enough time to get hidden or disguised.

The bouncing and jerking of the drive lasted another ten minutes, causing pain to slice through his lower body. As they approached the gate, he let out a deep breath. They were almost free.

In the passenger seat, a black book sat next to the gearshift. Pulling it open, he angled it in the moonlight to see a grainy picture of a man. Wouldn't do if Rashid's men looked close, but it was better than being in that hole.

The guard let the box truck through. It turned left, going back upriver and to the gated compound.

"ID?"

He handed the book over with a huff, hoping his anger would dissuade the guard from asking too many questions.

"What do you have?"

"Clothes. We found clothes in the water, and I'm supposed to take them upriver to the dogs. We can't find them here." He worked his accent, hoping to hide the American drawl that always seemed to come out.

The guard nodded as he walked to the back of the Jeep, pushing at the duffle bags. The guard pulled out the janitor's suit from the back, still dripping blood.

"Might not be alive to be worth the trouble." The guard chuckled.

Returning to the front, he handed Kenton the book and sent him through.

He turned right on the road and sped up, looking for the train crossing. The train's horn echoed in the air. He needed to get over the tracks to put space between them and Rashid.

The road appeared in the headlights, and he swung left. The light of the train engine shone in the distance, and he hit the accelerator.

Marcus appeared next to him.

"Hang on, Marcus. This is going to be close," he yelled over the engine and the sound of the train.

Gunfire erupted from behind, but he ignored it and focused on the road. Bumping and jumping back and forth, he struggled to stay upright while maintaining their speed.

Blasting through the wooden guardrails, the truck gained air before slamming into the ground on the other side. As they fishtailed, the wind of the train blasting past made him shudder.

"Well, not so close."

He laughed at Marcus. "What do you call close?"

"Been much closer." Marcus patted him on the shoulder. "Now, we need to have a discussion, Kenton."

He laughed again, straightening the truck and driving down the road to freedom.

1

Nine Years Later

"What do you mean, polished?" Her Yorkshire accent thickened as she glared at the older man behind the desk, the apparent ruler of her world at the moment.

"Don't take it that way, love. You know I value your abilities, and the fact you've learned so much in such a short time proves you're right where you need to be."

Olivia Lloyd frowned at her uncle, irritated at his need to put her in her place. Being her boss didn't entitle him to take over her life.

"If you had stayed, I'm not sure you would be as happy as you are here."

"I was doing what I loved before you stepped in."

"You and I both know you wouldn't have enjoyed where that road would take you."

She huffed. "You mean you wouldn't approve of where the road would lead. I've already emailed a friend of mine. I can re-enlist as an officer. I'd pass the test and return as a Second

Lieutenant. I believe within a year, I would become Lieutenant."

"No more working here with me?"

She rolled her eyes. "Working here with you has been good. But the action of military, I ... Can't you see that's what I need? This life is stifling, boring. And being in the States is ..." she trailed off, unable to finish that sentence.

"Lonely?"

Cutting a glare at her uncle, she stood.

"Olivia, you do realize telling me all this now is the worst possible timing. Our job here is in jeopardy."

"Yes, I know it's bad. But I wasn't going to let you know afterward. I've thought this over, and now that I have confirmation I can re-enlist, I'll be leaving for the UK next week. I have an appointment next Friday with my former CO. I'm headed back. That's the bottom line here." She turned and strode to the door. Gripping the knob, she paused. "I've got rounds to make, and then I'll be headed to lunch."

Ignoring his stern glare, she left the room before he could offer a rebuttal.

Gripping her keys, Olivia scanned the parking garage as she stepped off the elevator. Her heels clicking across the cement echoed, and she paused. Fingering the holster at her side, she reached her car, unlocking the door and sliding inside.

Starting the engine, she scanned the area. Someone was there, watching.

"Must be a lonely voyeur." She rolled her shoulders and backed out, turning onto the busy street and heading home.

Tapping the wheel, she let out a slow breath. Fighting with her uncle always came with guilt. He had done so much for her and was basically an adopted father. Although, he did have a habit of sticking his nose where it didn't belong.

But this job was never the plan. Moving to the States and working in the largest city in Texas, of all places, was never on her radar. Offering security detail for a high-tech company wasn't exactly a thrill. She'd been involved in one of the top training programs, the special armed services in Britain, and now she watched monitors and maintained security within the building.

She should've stayed in the military.

The ache of missing Daniel hit again. Another failed plan.

Why did everything go wrong?

Checking her mirrors, she took the exit to the large, lonely estate.

Her uncle had been right. She was lonely. Devastatingly lonely.

The sudden jolt of being hit from behind sent her head into the deployed airbag. Ringing echoed in her ears as spots danced across her unfocused vision.

Metal cracked, and the smell of fumes and gasoline filled the air. The car had stopped, which meant she needed to move. Unbuckling her seatbelt, she reached for the gun mounted next to her right leg.

She shoved it down to chamber a round, and as the heated breeze hit her skin, turned to see a masked man yanking on her arm.

"Let go," she hissed, but the man kept pulling.

Gritting her teeth and ignoring the bitter taste of blood, she wrenched her hand up, firing her weapon and hitting the first man square in the chest.

He fell back, and she flew from the car, searching the area and centering on the large SUV behind her still running.

"Get her!"

Movement to her left made her dive to the right as gunshots

resounded. Peering from over the hood of her car, she returned fire. Someone was set up on the other side of the road, hiding behind a parked car.

Two men slid from the van, one yelling, "Stop shooting! She's no good to us dead!"

She smirked and swung her gun around, narrowly missing a man with an assault rifle. If they wanted her alive, they were going to pay the price. The assailant from across the street hustled toward the SUV.

Yanking open the passenger door, she pulled an extra clip from the glove box and made her way toward the SUV, shooting and pushing them back. They dove behind the SUV as she dropped the empty clip and reloaded smoothly.

But she'd turned her back to her car. A sudden burn and sting made her scream, gun dropping as her world turned black and her body went weightless.

2

———

"Man, you have got to get it together."

Detective Kenton Matthews glared at his partner, Bruno Price, over his coffee cup. "What're you talking about now?" He grunted.

"I've seen that look before. You're thinking about dropping her."

He shook his head as Bruno collapsed in a chair at the break room table.

"Stay out of it, Brune."

"Milly is hot and smart. I have no idea how you end up with these women, but you've got to stop being so picky and just go for it."

He chuckled as he leaned a shoulder against the wall. "Go for it, huh? You think I'm looking at getting married?"

"At your age? Well, yeah. That's kinda the end goal, right?"

He frowned.

"There's nothing wrong with her. You're like a bad rerun of *Seinfeld* episodes. You find a problem with every single woman you meet and end up dumping her for something stupid."

He turned with a smirk. "I've never dated a woman with man-hands or an Elmer Fudd laugh."

Bruno laughed as Kenton sat down across from him.

"But we did break up yesterday."

Bruno paused mid-laugh and glared at him. "Seriously?"

Kenton set his coffee cup down with a shrug. "She's too smart for me. Besides, we have nothing in common. It was mutual. The second I brought it up, she said she had been thinking the same thing. Attraction is great and all, but if we have nothing in common, nothing to talk about, then there's not much left to do."

Bruno smirked. "There's always more to do."

"You're married," he said flatly.

Bruno chuckled. "I am." He sat back with a sigh. "Your problem is you keep meeting these women at the courthouse. Milly was there testifying on behalf of a friend, Shelly was there as a witness and was—"

"She had some emotional issues. Leave it at that." He'd tried to forget the way she cried at everything the few times they went out.

"Oh, but Karen. Now, she was great."

"She was a lawyer who wanted to win every discussion and argument. I couldn't even talk to her about anything because she made it a competition."

"See, too picky."

"I need you two for a minute." Captain Post motioned through the doorway.

Following Bruno, Kenton rotated his neck and rolled his shoulders. His morning workout hadn't loosened his joints, and his body was stiff and sore.

"You good?"

He nodded at Post as he sat next to Bruno.

"Getting stiff, old man?"

He smirked at the grin on Bruno's face. "This old man put you on the mat in record time yesterday."

"We were boxing, not that ninja stuff you know."

He chuckled. "A fight is a fight, and you lost."

"Gentlemen."

Kenton turned his gaze to Post.

"I've been asked to assign two agents on a threat. I've picked you two if you think you can stop bickering long enough to take a look."

Post handed each of them a binder. Not their usual form of communication.

"The Reliance Institute? You mean that tech company that has every kind of spyware and gadgets? Like James Bond?"

Kenton scoffed. "That's all fake. You know that, right?"

"Did you know—"

Post cleared his throat. "Gentlemen, this is a delicate situation. There's been an online threat against their company, and they are taking it very seriously. Although this company has board members from the UK, there are also a few Americans involved, and they want a police presence."

Kenton frowned. "They have some of the best security in the world. Why us? The feds probably have better clearance and allotment for this sort of thing."

"They do, but the company doesn't want clearance. They don't want us to get even a picture of what they have, so we're not going in to guard merchandise. We're doing a sweep, a terrorist assessment plan to fulfill the board members' wishes."

Kenton tossed the folder on the desk. "This is a brown-nosing mission, and I'm out. I don't need to waste my time satisfying someone's request to have an American step in and tell them they're doing a good job."

"I'm in."

His glare snapped to Bruno. "What?"

"Even if I don't get a peek at the goods they have in there, I can at least get inside. This is a tech-lover's fantasy, Ken. You have no idea."

Kenton shook his head and stood.

"Matthews, this isn't a request."

He paused. "Sir, with all due respect, it's not my job to go in just because they want a police officer's opinion or presence. We won't really be helping, and nothing we say will be considered. I have actual situations that need my attention."

"Price, give us a minute."

Kenton clenched his jaw as Bruno left, closing the door behind him.

"Have a seat, Matthews."

"I can stand, sir."

Post sighed heavily. "You have to make things so hard?"

"Sir—"

"Don't." Post held his hand up. "I was only to mention this if necessary, and considering they gave me the information, they must know you better than I do."

"Who's they?"

Post frowned. "You, specifically, were requested. It wasn't just the Americans that wanted the police. When met with the request, their chief information officer asked for you by name."

Kenton crossed his arms and racked his brain. No name emerged. He knew no one working in that kind of industry. "Who?"

"Marcus Moore."

Kenton's heart pounded as the memory flashed. "Moore? He lives here?"

Post shrugged and glared. "I only know he's in town and requested you." Obviously, being left out of the loop was bothersome. "Anything you want to say?"

"Classified, sir." With a grunt, Kenton grabbed the binder from the desk.

"They're expecting you at one, allowing you some time to get a few ideas based on what's in that book."

"Yeah, we'll be there." He headed out of the office.

Tossing the binder on his desk, he rushed past Bruno to the men's locker rooms.

Pacing a moment, he closed his eyes and tried to breathe through the vision of blood, the sound of gunfire, the pain. That was the moment. God used that precise moment to let him know he was not invincible and that his life had more than one purpose.

And He used Marcus Moore to do it.

Leaning against the wall, Kenton opened his eyes and let the shudder roll through. It didn't happen often, but on occasion, the nightmare returned. If he had done things differently ... Well, that wouldn't happen. He did the right thing, even though it almost cost him his life.

"Hey." Bruno stood a few feet away, leaning against the opposite wall with his arms crossed. "You were looking at me, but I don't think you saw me."

Kenton shook his head. "Just thinking."

Bruno knew about his previous career, but the details weren't something to discuss. They'd worked together for three years, and he hadn't had a flashback at work. Until now.

"That bad?"

He blew out a deep breath. "I'm good. Just needed a breather. I'm in on the op, by the way."

"Case. We call them cases."

He chuckled at Bruno's smirk. "Well, it's not a case, nothing's been taken. It's a consult of sorts, I guess."

"Yeah, consult. Sounds good. Meet you out there?"

He nodded as Bruno left.

God, what's the plan here?

Dizzy, he splashed his face with water. Taking a few deep breaths, he dried off and made his way to his desk.

"You think the threat is real?"

Kenton nodded. "I do. I know the chief information officer. If he requested me, there's something else going on. Find all the loose ends, Bruno. I want a list of things to give them."

Bruno grinned as he looked up from his computer. "I've already started."

Kenton chuckled and flipped past the electronic security. That was Bruno's area of expertise.

Going through the set-up of the company and perimeters of surveillance, he made a few notes. Although, most of what he could help with needed a more hands-on approach. It would have to wait until one.

Sitting back in his chair, he wondered why. Why, after all these years, would Marcus request him?

WALKING up the steps to the Institute, Kenton shook his head at Bruno. "You need to calm down."

"You just don't get it, man." The guy's smile was a mile wide.

Kenton sighed and led the way inside, finding an armed guard waiting. With little talk, they were led to an elevator and up to the top floor. Escorted to a room at the end of a long hall, they waited outside the closed door.

"Come in." A husky voice sounded as a click echoed.

They stepped through the door and entered the large, formal room. Sitting behind a desk was a familiar, smiling face.

Much older, grayer, but familiar.

3

"I've waited years to see you." Marcus Moore smiled as he walked around the desk.

It took Kenton a moment to engage as the man approached.

"I still don't believe it." He shook Marcus's hand. "He told me you were here, but I didn't believe it. Not till I saw you." He smiled as Marcus squeezed his hand with both of his.

"Old friends are hard to come by in our business. I'm glad you responded." Marcus's accent was still there, although not as thick.

"He almost didn't. Your name is the only reason he's here. I'm here because I wanted to be."

Kenton frowned at Bruno's wit. "Marcus, this is my partner, Bruno Price. He doesn't look like much, but he does good work with the tech side."

Bruno glared as they shook hands.

"I'm sorry, son, didn't mean to leave you out. Please have a seat."

Kenton watched Marcus make his way around the desk. For what he had endured and his age, he looked to be moving well.

"I was told you're not normally in town." He sat on the edge of the chair as Marcus took his seat at the desk with a nod.

"Yes, I live … elsewhere." He smirked, waving airily. "But after vetting the risk, I decided to step in. I believe an old friend of ours is making waves."

Kenton stood, heart pounding. "You're kidding," he growled.

Marcus shook his head as Kenton stood to pace.

"Sorry, can you be more specific? I'm apparently not privy to whatever connects you two."

"Of course, Detective Price. The man I'm referring to is an old acquaintance of mine— ours, actually. Halil Rashid."

"I've heard that name."

Kenton waited. Bruno had a photographic memory, and once he realized—

"Wait, you mean you two—" Bruno looked between them. "Kenton? Are you kidding me?"

"Look, we're not getting into details, okay? The guy is evil and a threat. One I should've taken care of years ago."

"We both had that mission, Kenton. We both failed."

He shook his head. "What's the damage?"

"We have a new blockchain genealogy. We've found a way to break the chain."

"What?" Bruno's jaw dropped as he paled.

"I'm not the IT guy here. Explain." Kenton crossed his arms and waited for Bruno to take a breath.

"Blockchain is used in cryptocurrency. It's an online ledger. It keeps companies honest because once an entry is made, it can't be undone. Each block represents a new entry, and each block is consensus-driven. Several different computers connected to the network have to solve a mathematical equation. Once the computers agree on a solution, the block is then added to the chain.

"It's secure in that you can't take away from the chain, you can only add to it. The amount of computer nodes that would have to be hacked at once makes it impossible to crack. It also means companies can't go back and rewrite previous entries."

Kenton nodded. "So, now that you've created a way to break the chain, that compromises who?"

Marcus let out a sigh. "Anyone that uses the program. Art dealers, real estate investors, and larger banks."

"That's a lot of money. But what are you going to do with that information? Why did you develop it in the first place?" His eyes shifted to Marcus as he leaned back in his chair, steepling his fingers.

"In order to stop someone from breaking the chain, we need to know how it's done. Now that we understand how it works, what it takes, companies can create the proper protocols and assessments to make sure it doesn't happen."

Kenton's jaw tightened. "How did Rashid find out about it?"

"Actually, how do you know it's him? I'm assuming he didn't sign his name."

He frowned, glaring at the back of Bruno's head.

"No, of course not. In his email, one we've been able to decode but not trace, he mentions me by name."

Marcus picked up a piece of paper from the desk and handed it to Kenton.

My dearest Marcus,

It's been far too long. Although this company has always captured my attention, I now have another purpose for making contact. I am requesting the blockchain genealogy by Sunday, 12:01 AM, or I will take it and any other technology I find purposeful. You can release this one thing, or I'll take it all.

*Terribly sorry I missed you back in Turkey, but I'm more
than thrilled you made it out alive.*

"That's it? This is enough to determine the threat is from
Halil Rashid?"

"Trust me, it's him." He glared until Bruno gave a nod.
"Have you advertised this technology? How did he discover it?"

"An attempted server breach occurred three days ago. We
were able to shut it down, but he had someone gain access."
Marcus let out a sigh. "Nothing was taken and we were able to
sever all connections to the hack, but the information doesn't
have to be proven. We have a certain reputation in this industry.
Our competitors know us well enough that we don't have to put
fake information on our servers.

"Rashid wants the tech by Sunday, or he'll launch a full
attack on our system and take it and anything else he can find
by force. But with what we have in place, it's a miracle he got in
at all."

"Well, actually …"

Kenton turned to Bruno.

"I noticed an interesting thing when we stepped inside the
building. I was automatically connected to your WiFi. No
password needed."

"I assure you our connections within this building are
secure."

Kenton chuckled at the irritated look on Bruno's face.
"Something you want to share?"

"If I might use my laptop?"

Marcus nodded, and Bruno pulled his laptop from the bag
he carried. As his fingers flew over the keys, Marcus came up to
Kenton.

"You look well."

"You do too. I wasn't sure what to expect." He chuckled as
the man rubbed his chest.

"It hurts some, but overall, I think I'm doing well for an old man."

"I think you are."

"Okay, here's a look at what someone with access to your WiFi can do."

Kenton gazed over Bruno's shoulder as Marcus stood behind him. "What am I looking at?"

"Those are my emails," Marcus said as two armed guards rushed through the door.

"We were told there's a network breach in here?"

"That's all right, gentlemen. Just being proven wrong."

Kenton pushed at Bruno's shoulder, and he shut down the computer as the two men left the office.

"You see, connecting to the WiFi can give any hacker worth their salt access. Since I was in your office and connected, my computer can connect to yours. But I'm not a professional hacker, I just want you to understand. Someone who does that for a living, they could make some waves. I obviously was discovered pretty quickly, but a pro wouldn't be."

Marcus frowned and paced a few steps. "You're saying it could've been a visitor that day?"

Bruno shrugged. "Possibly, or new personnel. Did you have either the day of the breach?"

"I don't know, but I can check."

Marcus sat at his computer, and Kenton began to pace once more. He'd hoped Rashid was dead after all these years. Now the nightmare had caught up to him.

"You're going to have to explain some things, man," Bruno muttered.

He sighed and looked down at his partner. "Classified."

"Declassify it." Bruno glared, and Kenton shook his head.

Halil Rashid was a tech savant responsible for cyber-attacks all over the world for the past fifteen years. He was Turkish-born and -raised, came to America to attend college, and went straight for the jugular: the stock exchange.

He caused massive havoc on internal servers that could've crippled the economy fifteen years ago. Kenton had run into Rashid three times. The first two were incidental, and the last was a failed mission to take him out covertly.

"We had no visitors but three new employees."

"I would check them first, without their knowledge. It's been three days, and if they're smart, they would've deleted any trace of where they've been and what they looked at. But you might find something they missed."

Marcus nodded. "Why don't you start on that?"

"Seriously, sir?" Bruno almost choked out the words.

Marcus chuckled. "Of course. I'll make sure you've got all the access you need. I would like to take Kenton with me to look around."

"Sounds awesome."

Kenton patted Bruno on the back. "Don't let the pressure get to you."

"Shut up," Bruno said as he stood.

The door opened and another man entered.

"Detective Price, this is Monte Drone. He's our head of tech security here."

"So, you're the hack?" Drone frowned as Bruno grinned.

"Just showing the man the risks."

Drone smirked. "Come on, we need to talk."

Bruno followed Drone out the door as Marcus stood.

"So, shall we take a walk?"

Kenton nodded and followed Marcus out the door and through the back stairwell.

"We've got surveillance in all stairwells, running on timed loops. You can't just tape over and play. It goes off in different intervals determined by a computer system. If the screen runs when it's not supposed to, it lets the monitor know. If the screen gets turned off or on other than when the computer dictates, it also lets the monitor know."

"Seems you've thought of everything."

Marcus chuckled. "I'm sure you'll find it if I didn't."

"How did you find me?"

They came out on the next level, walking through the hallways with glass partitions. Nothing was hidden. It would be difficult for someone to sneak through anywhere and not be noticed.

"I've always known where you were, Kenton. I watched your career as I recovered and moved on. I was allowed to come back briefly but was quickly benched, my superiors thinking it was a bad idea."

He chuckled. "I'm sure they did. So, this was the next step?"

"Of course not. I searched around, trying to find my way back into the game."

"You missed it that much?"

The spy recon world was very small. Not that Kenton missed it. When he got out, he'd considered himself lucky to be alive.

"The thrill, the excitement. It's terrifying, of course, but going out like I did ... it made it harder to give up." Marcus's features tightened.

"It wasn't your fault. You were stabbed in the back and sold. It wasn't you being caught or lacking ability."

Marcus shrugged. "I realize that, but still, it was hard to step away. I did what I could, finding work in-country and out. When I started looking at backing out, this position fell into my lap."

"I'm sure it did."

There was probably much more to that story.

They paused in front of a wall of mirrors, and he looked at the ceiling. The cameras were few, but with the mirrors, they could find all the corners, leaving no blind spots.

"You've got a security room on each floor?" He pointed at the mirrored wall as Marcus' eyebrow rose. "It's a little obvious, don't you think?"

Marcus chuckled. "Well, can't fool a recon specialist, I guess. Let me introduce you to a few people."

They passed through a door to find a set of monitors and surveillance equipment.

"Where's Ollie?"

A man turned and then stood quickly. "Um, lunch."

Marcus frowned. "Kenton, this is Glen Baxter. He's our second in command. The first seems to be at lunch."

He nodded at the man and followed Marcus into the hallway. "What about at night?"

Marcus paused, pushing his hands into his pockets. "We keep tech up twenty-four-seven. It's monitored on-site, never off. We pay for the best protection, and I'd like to think we've got it. But we both know how unhinged Rashid can be."

He nodded, face heating. "I should've—"

"Now, Kenton, we can't go through this again. I just want you to know, I debated even calling you in. But since you know how he thinks, how he works, I wanted your opinion."

Kenton sighed. "Can you remove the data that's going to be compromised?"

Marcus glared at him. "You can't be serious."

"If you want to be certain it's safe." He shrugged. "I'm not sure Bruno and I can offer anything you've not already thought of that will guarantee the info won't be breached."

Marcus shook his head. "Removing it is out of the question. Besides, we both know it could be a ploy to get some other technology, and he's sending us a false lead to leave us looking one way while he attacks from another."

"You've got a lot of good things set up here. Can I take a look outside? Especially the roof."

"The roof? I'm pretty sure that's out of the question. There's no access from outside. The exterior walls won't allow for any kind of attachment, and even the roof has a grid across it."

"Then let's go see." He grinned when Marcus nodded. "Follow me."

Once on the roof, he noticed the surveillance that would trigger an alarm should anything try to land.

"If I were to use this as an access point, it would be perfect."

"How do you mean?" Marcus crossed his arms.

"You lock that door, and I've got all the time in the world up here. We both know he doesn't need much time to get whatever he wants. I can disable that door, and no one could approach me since it's the only one. The alarms, yes, but he would be able to divert them for at least a little while. Even if they did go off, what could you do except wait for a police helicopter?"

Marcus glanced between him and the door with a frown. "I see your point. So, now what?"

He measured the distance from the stairwell door to the end of the building. "I don't have a blueprint."

Marcus retrieved his phone and pulled up the building plans, handing him the phone. Kenton scrolled through to the top floor. "There's a room full of computers below me, right?"

Marcus nodded.

"At night, you said all your surveillance is in-house. How many people do you keep on staff at night?"

"Ten. Two security officers on the ground floor and the rest monitor the systems and the building."

"Can you access the room below me? I want to see a live feed."

Marcus took the phone and tapped the screen several times before returning it.

"Okay, the sun creates a glare on the glass, you see?" He held the phone for Marcus. "The moon at its fullest and with no clouds will make the same kind of glare. I can't even see the person at this terminal. If it's nighttime, and I know no one is supposed to be at that desk, I'll assume no one is there.

"He can find a way to disconnect the sensors here. We both know how easy it is to rappel into that room in the glare. It's all dependent on the variables, but then again, that's how we work." He grinned. "How we used to work."

Marcus frowned and paced a moment. "You've found the key, I think," he mumbled.

"Is there no other access besides being on-site?"

Marcus shook his head.

"Then how do you keep track from where you live?"

"I see your point, but I'm not the enemy."

"You're not. But knowing Rashid, you're a perfect patsy. You're the only one with remote access, and I bet he knows that by now." Handing the phone back to Marcus, he frowned. "I'm serious, Marcus. You need to take precautions at home. He has a vendetta, and although I assumed he would have moved on, that email indicates he's targeting you."

Marcus nodded. "You're right. I need to make some calls. Come on. We'll wait for your partner in my office."

4

———

As Kenton and Marcus headed back to the office, Marcus kept trying to make a call on his phone. He grunted and shook his head as he rounded his desk, the phone to his ear.

"Ollie?" Marcus's body stiffened, his hand falling to the desk. "Okay, I've got it." Hanging up with a smile, Marcus glanced at the cameras

Kenton's eyebrow went up. "You good?"

Marcus's smile got bigger. "I found Ollie. Now, let's get you and your partner out of here. I'm sure you're famished. Probably ready to go eat, and we have great food trucks around here."

Grabbing the phone next to his computer, Marcus pushed a button. "Let's get Detective Price back to the lobby, please."

Marcus smiled and walked around the desk, reaching out to shake his hand. "It was good to see you. Just like old times."

Kenton put on a smile. "Old times. I'll talk with you later, Marcus." He nodded and left the office, following the waiting escort from the hallway into the elevator and then to the lobby.

Bruno showed up with a frown, huffing as he came from the

elevators. "What's going on? I was knee-deep in the most amazing technology."

"We have to go. Come on." He refrained from running, although every nerve ending told him he had to hurry. He ignored Bruno's agitation as they got in the car and started it up. "Find the nearest food truck."

"What?"

"Bruno," he growled. "Find the nearest food truck. I won't ask again."

"Easy, man. There are a few around the corner."

He hit the gas, pulling through the light and into the lot. Three food trucks were set up and open.

"Wait here and don't move," he said as he got out.

Pretending to look at his phone, he studied each truck. Zeroing in on the last truck, he noticed a red scarf wrapped around the awning's metal arm.

Striding to the truck, he put on a smile and waited in line for a few minutes.

"Can I help you?"

"Yeah, order for Mason."

Just saying the name from nine years ago made his heartbeat spike.

The woman looked him up and down, then went to the back. She returned with a sack containing several Styrofoam containers.

"Twenty."

He handed over the cash and headed to the car.

Bruno took the sack with a sigh. "Okay, man. What's up?"

"You say a word, and I'll know who to come after."

"What? What in the world is going on?"

"Marcus and I met when I pulled him out of a situation almost ten years ago. He's SAS."

"What? Like James Bond?"

He grunted. "No jokes. He took a call. He's got something going on. Whoever Ollie is, that's what's going down."

"Down as in, someone is involved in a spy game with the former spy?"

Pulling into their station's parking lot, he slammed the car into park and took the bag. Opening the first container, he found a phone and scrolled through.

"This is a mirrored phone of Marcus's." He hit the most recent call.

"Ollie?" Marcus's voice came through the phone, just like in the office.

"She's otherwise detained." A low voice rumbled over a scream in the background. "We want the blockchain code. Send it to your laptop within the hour, or she dies."

"Don't—" The woman's voice was cut off by a slap.

"Okay, I've got it."

The call ended.

"Who has that woman?" Bruno's face paled.

"We're going to find out. Marcus will give up the code if we don't take care of it first."

"We? We can't take care of it. This is SWAT territory."

"She dies in less than an hour. There's no time to go through all the channels, get the teams set up, find the house."

Opening the next Styrofoam box, Kenton discovered a small envelope that held blueprints of a house, a few different entrances marked with key codes.

"I'm going in. You need to stay here."

Rushing from the sedan, he sprinted to his SUV and opened the back as he shrugged off his jacket. As he slid on the tactical vest and loaded the pockets with gear, Bruno came up next to him.

"Look, I'm there. But this isn't our territory. We do risk assessments."

"What do you think I used to do while in the Army?"

Bruno shrugged. "I looked you up. Lots of redacted files and stuff."

He frowned. "You're a smart guy. Figure it out."

Grabbing the backpack, he opened the sedan door and took out the details of the house and his phone.

"You were a spy?" Bruno whispered as he followed him back to the SUV.

"No, the Army doesn't have spies." He loaded up, and the passenger door opened, Bruno sliding into the seat. Kenton studied him for a moment. "You sure?"

"I'll take care of the security." He pulled his laptop inside with him. "I saw codes?"

He handed Bruno the list as he backed out and headed to the address. "He said he didn't live around here. This must be a safe house."

"So, who is Ollie?"

"No idea."

"How well do you know this guy?"

Kenton sighed. "You ask too many questions. Like I said, no one can know the connection, and no one needs to know about Moore. You give that up, we don't talk again."

"I get it, man. You can trust me."

Bruno was a good partner, but he often spoke before he thought. Just as in the office earlier with Marcus, his quick wit had always been an issue.

"Oh, man."

"What?"

"I got into the video feed. It's not good."

Slamming his brakes at a stop light, he looked at the screen. A woman was bound with tape over her mouth and all four limbs secured to the legs of a chair. Three men roamed around her as one stayed focused on the computer screen.

"They can see him. He glanced at the cameras before I left. He does something to let them think he's sending help, they'll kill her."

Kenton hit the gas. They were running low on time.

5

———————

As they neared the exit for the address, Kenton frowned at the police tape fluttering in the wind.

A silver car sat on one side, the back fender crushed in and front doors wide open. The smell of gunpowder still hung in the air.

"This is a high-end area. I wonder if whatever happened to Ollie started out this far." He glanced at Bruno.

"I'm looking it up now."

Parking half a mile from the house on the map, Kenton pulled to the side of the road and studied the plans Marcus left him.

"Looks like that car is registered to a Slade Jefferson. The police found lots of shell casings and blood. No witnesses, and they've yet to find Jefferson."

"Jefferson was an alias of Marcus's. Back there is where she was taken. Let's just hope she's not too badly injured." He handed the plans to Bruno. "I'll go here first, then there second." He pointed to the entries as he pulled his rifle from the back seat.

"What if I need to talk to you?"

"You can't. I'll go left."

"What?'

He groaned. "If I come to a fork, I'll go left. Cover my left, and you'll be able to help me out."

Sprinting through the field, he arrived at a gated drive. The brick fence around the estate stood at least eight feet tall. He backed up, hoping the cameras wouldn't pick him up, and sprinted across the drive.

The tall brick wall surrounding the estate had mounted lights and alternating cameras.

"Better have my back," he muttered as he centered under a camera, backed away several feet, and took a run at the wall.

Using long-forgotten skills triggered his muscle memory to take over, and he made his way atop the wall as the camera paused, flashing red for the few seconds it took him to clear it. With a grin, he jumped inside the fence to the first entry.

The lock disengaged as soon as he stepped up, the camera pausing its scan. Stepping through the door, he found himself in the basement. Taking the first left, he slid along the wall, keeping out of sight in the darkened area.

He lingered by the water heater in the back corner and opened the door to the pilot light. Grabbing a crate, he set it as close as possible to the exposed flame. Expelling a bullet from the chamber of his gun, he placed it upright on the crate next to the flame.

Continuing to a staircase, he slowly took the steps, working to be as light-footed as his former self. At the top, he eased open the door to the main house. Men's voices echoed in the hallway, and he frowned.

He stepped into the hallway to his left and paused just outside the main room. He needed a distraction while his bullet heated. Slinking back through the house, he propped open the basement door, then hid in a small closet under the stairwell.

Tapping his knife gently on the floor, he waited.

"Just go."

Footsteps echoed, then paused.

"Did you leave the door open?"

"No, of course not."

He smiled. Two for one. That meant only two left guarding the woman.

"Check it out."

"You."

An argument ensued, and he clenched his teeth, his patience running out. Peeking through the crack, Kenton saw one man holding the door to the basement. Easing out, he checked the empty hallway, then kicked the man inside, closing and locking the door.

Sprinting to the right, he took out the man waiting in the doorway and aimed around the corner to see the last man with a gun to the woman's head.

"Almost, but not quite."

"You're dead either way."

"So is she," the man hissed.

"No, I don't think so."

He waited a moment, praying the men hadn't found his trap yet. The pounding on the door would suggest they were otherwise occupied. The power suddenly went out, and the man's focus lapsed enough for him to take the shot.

The man dropped, and Kenton rushed to the woman, pulling out his phone and quickly removing the tape from her mouth.

"His number?"

"Six, nine, eight, seventy-two hundred," she whispered as he dialed.

Grabbing the other knife from its sheath, he removed the tape from her wrist, and she took the knife to complete the rest.

"Kenton?"

"She's safe."

"Thank goodness. I'm on my way."

"He's coming." Turning his attention to the woman, he found her ripping the remnants of the tape from her wrists and legs.

She grimaced as she stood, face bloodied and bruised. Looking to the cameras, he motioned for Bruno to come in. His phone vibrated against his chest. He shifted his rifle strap out of the way to answer.

"Yeah?"

"The two you left are coming around the side."

He hung up, pulled the woman's hand, and pushed her into the stairwell closet. "Don't move."

Slamming the door, he hid in the corner of the entry, waiting for the men to arrive.

A barrage of gunfire erupted, destroying the front door and sending wood flying across his face. The remnants of the door were kicked in, and he took out the leader in one shot, then aimed for the other.

A gunshot came from behind, and he ducked and turned. The other man fell forward as the woman lowered her weapon.

"You left your back exposed." Her British-laced accent hung in the air.

Kenton straightened as the slamming of a car door took his attention.

Bruno came running up the drive, gun in hand.

"We've got it."

"We?"

Kenton turned and motioned to the woman. "I'm assuming you're Ollie. Marcus's head of security."

She nodded tightly and shoved the gun in her waistband before marching toward the back of the house.

"Um?" Bruno's voice echoed.

Kenton shrugged and followed the woman. As he made his

way into the kitchen, he found his knife on the counter, her back to him as she filled a bag with ice from the freezer.

"Need help?'

"No." Clipped and stern but calm. "You know who I am. So, who are you?" She turned, setting the bag on her face with a wince.

Resting on a barstool, he grabbed his knife and put it back in the sheath at his chest, looking her over. There was something familiar about this woman. And something ... odd.

"I'm a detective."

She frowned. "I doubt that."

"No, he is. I'm Bruno, by the way. Bruno Price." Bruno held out his hand, which she hesitantly shook.

"You're really a detective?" Her eyes flitted between his and Bruno's.

"Are you from England?"

Kenton shook his head. Bruno had no tact. How he ever got a wife ...

"Yes, Yorkshire. Where are you from, Detective Price?"

"Here. I've lived here all my life."

It was her eyes. There was something familiar about her eyes. Hidden underneath all the red, they were an amazing green color. She wasn't crying. That's what seemed odd.

"Is this your first hostage situation, Ollie?"

Her eyes cut to his. "Why do you ask?"

"You seem very calm and in control for someone who was captured, taped up, and beaten."

She shrugged. "Part of the job."

He let out a smirk and shook his head. "No, I don't think so."

Her jaw set.

"Ollie?" Marcus's voice echoed through the house, and he soon appeared. "You ... what did they do?" He frowned as he rushed into the room, taking her elbows.

"I'm okay, really. You have amazing friends, Marcus."

Ollie's smile nearly bowled Kenton over. Even through the bruises and the redness, her smile lit her face.

Marcus wrapped her in a hug. "You don't know, dear. You really don't."

She leaned back, her eyes wide. "Really?"

Marcus nodded, and her gaze locked on Kenton's.

"You're Kenton Matthews?"

"And you are?"

Marcus chuckled. "Olivia Lloyd. My niece."

She stepped to Kenton, eyes narrowing. "I was expecting ... younger."

Bruno chuckled.

Kenton enjoyed the smug expression on her face, the way she studied him. "Is that your car on the highway we passed? Looks pretty bad. You sure you're alright?"

Her face went red. "Are you saying I'm weak?"

"I'm saying you saved my back. Thanks."

Her eyebrow rose a fraction as she turned back to Marcus. "What did you learn today?"

Marcus looked between them with a smirk. "Kenton had a lot to say, and I believe Drone will inform me Detective Price was also helpful. I am, however, more concerned about you." Marcus frowned as he lifted her chin to study her face.

"I'm fine."

"It doesn't look fine."

Her gaze cut Kenton from across the bar. "I am capable of taking care of myself."

"Hey, Ken?"

He lingered on Olivia for a moment before turning to Bruno.

"Why were you just standing there waiting earlier? Did you know I was going to cut the power?"

He shook his head as a gunshot rang through the house. Marcus pulled Olivia behind him, and Bruno hit the deck.

"Nope, waiting on that. Don't remember it taking so long." He stood and rotated his head.

"I think we've all had a busy day already. Perhaps a quiet night at home would help." Marcus looked over Olivia and then back to him.

Kenton nodded. "I'm free. I'd like to know what you've been up to."

Marcus chuckled and shook his head. "Now, you know that's not part of the conversation."

"Let's get out of here, Ken." Bruno stood from the floor as he straightened his shirt.

Kenton chuckled and followed Bruno out of the kitchen. "I'll be back later."

"Six thirty," Marcus called.

"Sounds good."

He patted Bruno on the back as they stepped past the rubble of the front door. "You know, with a little training, you'd make a great tech specialist for Recon."

He grinned as Bruno paled.

As he slid behind the SUV's wheel and pulled onto the road, his mind went to Olivia. She was beautiful and tough, considering the beating she took.

He sighed at the connection, his mind wandering as he strained to focus on the road.

Marcus Moore's niece. Man.

"What're they going to do? I mean, there are four dead men in their home."

"They'll call the police, report a kidnapping and home invasion. Olivia and Marcus defended themselves."

"That's lying, and we'll be involved in the lie."

He frowned and glanced over at his worried partner. "Never mind what I said. You'd make a terrible Recon tech specialist."

6

"So, that's the American you've raved about for years?" Olivia sat against the bar, holding the ice to her aching head.

Marcus relented his phone to his pocket. "Police will be here in ten, and yes, he's the man who saved my life."

"He's ... different than I expected."

Marcus chuckled. "Kenton Matthews is an interesting man. He's never let the work he did affect his life. Although, to be honest, he had a bad habit of doing what was right."

She frowned and stood to follow Marcus down the hallway. "What does that mean?"

"I need to call someone to fix the door."

"Marcus."

He turned and looked her over with a frown. "First, tell me how?"

Pulling up the back of her shirt, she winced as Marcus fingered the burn marks made by the taser.

"Where?"

"On the highway before the exit. They slammed into me

and attacked. One yelled that they needed me alive, and I took advantage. But miscounted."

Marcus nodded. "Left your back exposed."

"I thought it was clear. They were all in front of me." Her jaw tightened. "How did Kenton know to come?"

"They called me when he was in the room."

"And he just knew to come?"

Marcus sighed. "Love, our jobs consisted of working together, making the pieces fit when no one else could. It was like old times."

Letting out a sigh, she shook her head.

"Still feeling bored here in the States?" He shoved his hands in his pockets.

Rolling her eyes, she slammed the basement door shut and went to push the stairwell closet closed when something caught her eye.

Kneeling, she found a razor-sharp hunting knife on the floor. The initials KM were carved into the handle. As she turned it over, the initials MM were also carved. Standing, she pocketed the knife as sirens wailed in the distance.

<hr>

After dealing with the detectives and the cleaning crew, Olivia lay down on her bed with a sigh. She still ached even with the shower and a soak in the jet tub. A soft knock made her grunt as she sat up.

"Yes?"

"I wondered if you needed something for your face?"

She chuckled at Marcus as he walked into the room holding a steak. "No, I'm fine. I realize you believe that's the best thing, but I'm not keen on uncooked meat on my face."

He sighed and looked her over with a frown. "They did a job."

"Yeah, well, since I woke attached to the chair, I didn't have a fighting chance."

"I think we might need more lessons."

She frowned. "I wouldn't need more lessons if I were still working."

Marcus turned away as he sat next to her. "I couldn't let you go down that road, Ollie. You're all the family I have left."

She sighed and gave him a hug. "I know. I'm sorry. It's been a long day."

He hugged her back gently. "Nothing's broken?"

"No, nothing's broken."

"Good. Get some rest, and I'll call you for dinner."

As Marcus left, she laid back down and took a breath. Her mind numbing from the pain medicine, she drifted as the image of Kenton Matthews came to life. Tall and broad, those striking cobalt eyes intent.

Without even having to ask, Kenton came running. He came without pause, without knowing what waited for him behind the doors. He didn't even know who she was, but he came just because of Marcus.

After the police left, she'd scoured the security video. It showed nothing at first, the cameras going black as he entered the house. But moving through each camera angle, she finally found the footage of him coming over the large brick wall, then entering the house. He had no time to form a plan, to determine what needed to be done. He just did it. His skill and ability—well, his military training—had served him well.

With a sigh, she sat up. Even with all the training, her abilities seemed so limited. If given the same problem, she couldn't be certain she would be as successful as Kenton had been.

Not good enough for the SAS, not confident in her military career. Every path she chose faltered. Even bored out of her mind protecting the rich, she would still be there if Marcus hadn't convinced her to come here.

Maybe all of this was pushing her back into the military where she belonged, right? She could learn all she needed there. Become a better ... everything.

Pulling the knife from her nightstand, she turned it over in her hand. How did her uncle end up with the knife to carve his initials? Or was it her uncle's knife, and Kenton had ended up with it?

Setting it on her nightstand, she burrowed into the bed. Her body begged for rest, and the pounding of her head eased as she fell into sleep.

7

───────

Walking up to the front door, Kenton smiled to see it repaired as if nothing had happened. With Marcus's connections, he was confident the four men's deaths would be put to rest quickly, even though Kenton's gun had fired the bullets. Well, most of them.

He knocked and rotated his neck, feeling the effects of moving like a younger man.

Marcus grinned as he opened the door. "Kenton. Come in."

"Looks perfect. I take it you had no problems cleaning everything up?"

The smell of chemicals and bleach lingered in the air as Marcus shrugged.

"No problems. Ollie is still upstairs. I haven't woken her yet."

He nodded and followed Marcus to the kitchen.

"She took quite a few hits." Kenton sat on a barstool and leaned into the bar, grabbing a carrot slice off the tray.

"Yes, she did. She was always good at taking hits," he mumbled.

"That's a curious comment." He smirked as Marcus frowned.

"She wanted to do more. Ollie is very passionate, very resolved. When she found out about me, she was determined to follow in my footsteps. Something I tried hard to avoid."

The man pulled something that smelled amazing out of the oven.

"A spy who can cook?"

Marcus chuckled. "It calms me. I like creating sometimes instead of destroying." He rubbed his hands together.

"That's why I joined the force. Needed to make a difference without losing myself to the job."

Marcus leaned against the counter, crossing his arms. "Out of everyone I know, you losing yourself to the job seems unlikely."

Swallowing his bite, Kenton stood. "Water?"

Marcus motioned to the fridge. "Kenton, I know what you saw."

Taking a drink, Kenton settled next to the fridge. "When?"

Marcus's eyebrows went up.

He shook his head. "No, I don't think you did."

"It's the date that gives it away, I'm afraid. I was getting information about what was happening when you were there. We knew there was a possibility of an attack, and when I started looking for you and couldn't locate you, I assumed you were the one inside."

Kenton took another drink.

"Halil's son's birthday." Marcus shook his head and went to the fridge, pulling out a bottle of wine. "I tried that same route five years previous. Why do you think he went after me back then?"

"For the same reason he goes after anyone. He's evil."

Marcus chuckled. "Well, I was spotted. That's why I got out

and lost my chance. That intel must've moved on to your government, and you were sent in."

"I think that's enough work talk." He wanted to avoid the upcoming conversation.

"I agree. Wine?" Marcus poured two glasses of the red drink, and Kenton shook his head.

"Never been much on wine."

"Pity." He combined the glasses.

"Olivia doesn't like wine?"

"No. Her parents were killed by a drunk driver when she was young. She refuses even to try it." Marcus sighed. "When that happened, I was the only family able to care for her. No living grandparents and my sister-in-law's family never approved of my brother, so they didn't want to be involved. Considering my job, I thought it wise to hire a nanny and visit as often as was safe. But it was difficult. I worried all the time."

"She seems centered."

"Oh yes, that's the word." Marcus grinned before taking a sip. "She reminds me of someone." Marcus's eyebrows rose with a chuckle.

Kenton frowned. "No, I don't think so."

"You have no idea. She would give you a run, I imagine."

"No offense, but I'm not interested."

Marcus watched as Kenton sat back on his barstool and picked at the veggie tray.

"I think maybe you are. She's only a few years younger than you. Much too good for you, of course."

"Exactly." Kenton winked as Marcus laughed.

"Something you want to share?"

He turned with a smile and shook his head, trying to keep from reacting. Olivia's face, although bruised, looked great. The swollen mass he expected was gone.

"Your magic treatment works wonders." Marcus grinned as Olivia came around the bar and took a few carrots.

"Doesn't make it hurt less," she muttered.

Kenton chuckled and swigged his water, watching her avoid him at all costs.

"It's time to eat." Marcus clapped his hands and grabbed the dish he'd pulled from the oven before heading to the dining room.

He took the veggie tray from Olivia with a grin, and she narrowed her eyes. Waiting at the bar, he followed her around, enjoying the trip to the table where he set the tray next to the hot dish.

Marcus pulled out the chair for Olivia and sat at the head. Kenton sat across from her as Marcus reached for their hands. Red rushed to Olivia's cheeks, and he suppressed a grin, taking hold of Marcus's forearm. Her hand reached across for his and he took it, gripping her fingertips as he closed his eyes.

Marcus cleared his throat. "Lord, thank You for sending Your protection today. You knew what would happen and had it all handled before we could've reacted. Use this food to keep us strong and guide our steps. Amen."

Kenton kept hold of Olivia as Marcus said "amen," grinning as she pulled away.

Small talk between Olivia and Marcus severed the silence as they dished out the food. He sat back, listening to their conversation as he finished eating the delectable meal.

"Kenton, tell me how you ended up in Dallas with a local police department instead of a federal institute?" Marcus looked up with a smirk.

Kenton took a sip of his water. "I needed a move, and federal wasn't interesting to me. I wanted low-key."

"So, a detective? What kind of detective?" Olivia finally made eye contact, her bright green irises focused.

"I work terrorist threats. Anytime someone of importance comes to town and needs protection, I step in and assess the situation. Just like I did at Marcus's office today."

"Assessments? A former military man doing assessments? Aren't you bored out of your mind?"

He chuckled at her astonished expression. "Not bored. Alive. I made it out. I survived. I've had enough excitement in my lifetime. Besides, I'm not sure my body could take the kind of work I used to do."

Her eyes narrowed. "Marcus said you found something?"

"Roof. With Rashid's skills, he would have no problem rappelling from the roof to the room below. Access to the computers wouldn't be an issue. It's just a timing thing."

She looked unconvinced. "I highly doubt someone could gain access so quickly and efficiently with the security we have in place."

"He gave you a warning." He smirked as she nodded slowly.

"Yes, Sunday at midnight."

Marcus chuckled.

"Why do that?"

She huffed. "Because it wasn't a real threat? Because he wants us distracted with one thing to access another."

"His timing is perfect, always. Why attack you?" His eyebrow rose as her face reddened.

"That was an act of convenience." She sat back and crossed her arms.

He leaned forward. "No, he knew exactly what he was doing. He's proving he can get the information from different aspects. He knew there was access from an outside computer. He knew about at least one of Marcus's safe houses and saw you as a means to an end. Rashid is skilled, has money to hire the best, and doesn't care who he hurts in the process." He narrowed his gaze. "I suggest you move to a safer location."

"That's already been arranged. We'll have a car here at eight."

Kenton nodded at Marcus, his eyes never leaving hers. "Good. That won't be the last attempt, I'm sure."

She took a drink of water and stood, collecting her plate and gliding to the kitchen.

"I think she got the drift."

Kenton frowned as his gaze tracked her, then turned to Marcus. "She'll be targeted again. You know that. She's here with you and—"

"And now she and I will stay in the same house. She's been living here by herself for six months. I'm moving her into my home until this all clears up."

Kenton nodded.

"How about we have a dessert on the deck?"

Kenton stood and took his plate, just to have Marcus retrieve it from him with a smile.

"I've got this. You go wait for me."

Stepping outside to the back deck, he smiled as Olivia followed.

"I have a question." She leaned against the brick partition with her arms crossed.

The wind fluttered her yellow blouse and pulled strands of light brown hair around her face. She wore dress slacks neatly fitted to her trim legs that reminded him how tall she was. Even in flat sandals, she stood right at his shoulder. She carried herself well, as though she knew she was beautiful.

"Okay."

Her eyebrow rose. "So, you'll answer me?"

"I can try."

She stood from the wall and tilted her head, those green eyes searching. "How old are you?"

He chuckled. "That's your question?"

She shook her head. "No, but you're just not what I expected."

He pushed into her space. She met his gaze, never flinching or tensing up.

"How old do you think I am?"

She shrugged, her eyes moving to his chest for a moment. "I don't know."

As she started to turn, he took hold of her elbow. She smirked over her shoulder.

"I've heard stories. The way Marcus talks about you, I assumed you were his age or perhaps a little younger. Mid- to late-forties, at least."

He chuckled. "Nope, that's a little older than me."

"I know. It's just the stories." She shook her head.

"I'm thirty-eight, Olivia."

Her eyebrow rose. "I go by Ollie."

"I know."

With a frown, she pulled from his grip. He sighed and watched her walk away. Pocketing his hands, he took a deep breath. Her floral perfume floated back as he smiled at her retreating figure.

What was he getting himself into?

"So, you'll answer?"

He pulled his gaze to her face as she started to turn. "If I can."

Surprise flashed in her eyes. Reaching behind her back and lifting her blouse slightly, she pulled his knife from her waistband.

He grinned and stepped closer. "I was hoping it was here and the police didn't take it." As he reached, she held it up.

"I have questions."

He nodded and stepped back, sitting against the brick partition and crossing his arms. "Did you ask Marcus?"

She shook her head.

"Why not?"

Her mouth pulled to the side. "Marcus tends to hide things from me. I believe he thinks telling me all the details will make me ... I don't know, want to do something more."

"Or maybe the details are not something for him to repeat."

She stepped closer, focusing on the knife while he couldn't take his eyes off her.

"You're initials and his. Whose knife is it?" Her green eyes flicked to his, making him grin like an idiot.

"It was mine first."

She smiled.

Man.

"When did my uncle have it?" She settled beside him against the wall, her perfume enveloping him.

"I lent it to him when we first met."

She nodded. "So, he kept it? Added his initials?"

He took a breath and glanced at the windows, wondering where Marcus was watching from.

"He's not coming out."

His gaze cut to her. "Why not?"

"I think he received a phone call."

He leaned closer. "But that doesn't mean he's not watching us."

She chuckled. "Yes, he's a good spy."

"After we met."

"After you saved him." Her green eyes brightened, making him smirk.

"When we met, I lent it to him. When we parted, getting my knife back wasn't a thought or priority."

She inched closer, making him shake his head as he diverted his attention once again to the house, his heartbeat jumping up a notch.

"So, when did you see him to get it back?"

"He hasn't shared that with you?"

She shook her head, her brown hair falling over her shoulders. Leaning toward her, he smiled.

"Then I won't share that either."

Her eyes narrowed as a smirk crossed her face. "How close did I come?"

He chuckled. "Closer than I'd like to admit."

She stood, holding the knife in her palm. "It's an amazing knife. Well weighted." Her eyes flashed to his for a second, then she turned and flicked the knife over her shoulder. It sank into the crossbeams of the window.

He smiled. "I've noticed."

She nodded, then glided back inside.

Blowing out a deep breath, he shook his head. She was good. Whatever group she'd trained with—SAS, intelligence, military—had trained her well. He would like to think it wasn't all an act.

He chuckled. Man, he really wanted to believe that.

While Kenton tried to ease his pounding heart, Marcus came out and paused at the knife sticking into the narrow wooden slats. He shook his head and pulled up on the knife, holding it in his hand as he admired it.

"I suppose she found this?"

Kenton nodded.

"What did you tell her?"

"She asked whose it was and then how you got it."

"That's all?"

"And how I got it back."

Marcus chuckled. "I've not shared that story."

"I didn't either."

Marcus's eyes went wide. "Really? She's very convincing. I always have to be prepared when working my way out of storytelling."

He laughed and raked his fingers through his hair. "She was ... close."

Marcus handed him the knife. "I haven't thanked you enough for saving her."

Kenton took the knife and pulled up his jeans at the ankle. He pushed the weapon through the empty sheath and eased the jeans back down. "You don't have to thank me. We've been through too much, had each other's backs too often to say thanks." He stood as Marcus took his arm.

"This is different. She's like my daughter. I can't always be around, and I—"

"Marcus." He turned to face his friend. "Don't ask me to do something I can't promise."

Marcus frowned but nodded.

"You can call me anytime. Either of you. If you need help, call me. But don't ask a duty I can't complete."

"Of course." Marcus sighed heavily. "Today almost killed me. To hear her scream."

He gripped Marcus's shoulder. "I was there, too, and I didn't even know her."

Marcus nodded, his face dropping as his shoulders fell. "Well, let's not dwell on this further. I think it's time for some dessert."

8

Kenton made quick work of the strawberry trifle Marcus had prepared before standing to leave. With Olivia's demeanor turning unfriendly by the time they finished dessert, he figured he had worn out his welcome.

"I appreciate the invite to dinner. Everything was delicious." He headed to the front door, Marcus in the lead.

"I'm off to pack. See you in the morning, Detective Matthews." Her pointed stare made him nod as she ascended the staircase.

He did his best to keep from watching, but she was mesmerizing. Shaking his head, he turned to exit through the door Marcus had opened and joined him on the porch.

"You seem ... different."

Kenton chuckled at Marcus's assessment. "No, I'm not the same. I don't guess I'll ever be the same after everything we went through. But I am thankful."

"Thankful?" Marcus crossed his arms.

"If I hadn't met you, I might never have come to know Christ."

Marcus chuckled. "You know that's not how it works. He can send anyone to give the good news to others."

He shrugged. "Yeah, but in that situation, at that time in my life, I'm not sure I would've been convinced without the situation we survived. Feeling as if you're going to die changes how you perceive your life."

Marcus nodded, glancing back at the door. "Finding someone to share your life with can do the same. Trust me."

Kenton's smile slipped as he shook his head. "No acts of promise. I won't do that."

"I don't think I'll have to ask."

His gaze jumped to Marcus, finding his stare that brought back memories. Intense and in control, Marcus had brought him through many things in his life, giving him wisdom and strength previously unknown.

But right now, if Marcus was expecting something more between him and Olivia, he would be disappointed.

"Good night, Marcus."

"See you in the morning."

He hurried to the SUV, unwilling to get into further discussion about the man's beautiful and talented niece.

<hr>

As Olivia packed her bag, she groaned. Even with the pain medication and globs of makeup, she looked and felt pained.

Sitting on the edge of the bed, she pulled up her email on her phone, fingers hovering above the one from her former classmate, now a Second Lieutenant in the Army. He'd convinced her to rejoin. If only she hadn't quit in the first place. With a sigh, she pushed the phone back into her pocket.

Shoving her clothes into the bag, she zipped it up and slammed it to the floor.

"You ready, love?"

"Yes, I'll be right down."

Yanking her overnight bag onto her shoulder, she pulled her suitcase behind her to the stairs.

"Let's go. The car is waiting." Marcus climbed the stairs and took the suitcase. She followed him down the steps and out the door.

Once settled in the car, Marcus turned to her. "Let's discuss this re-up campaign."

"I'm going back. I never should've left in the first place."

"Olivia, you left because it wasn't what you wanted in life. You wanted more. Settling back into that role won't satisfy you."

"Then what else am I to do?"

He grinned. "Stay here. Continue working for me. It could lead to other contacts, other job opportunities."

Studying her uncle, she licked her lips. "What other opportunities?"

"This is a big country, and we already have a lot of contacts." He took her hand. "You didn't like the military, and you didn't enjoy the private sector overseas. But those things are much different here. Perhaps you'll find another avenue to fill your time."

"Do you honestly think I wouldn't have made it in the SAS?"

Marcus frowned. "You're much too good of a person. What it takes to do that kind of work is not all as it seems."

She patted his hand. "You're a good person, Uncle Marcus. After all, God still has you here, working and doing good."

"God has left me here for a reason. I just hope in all my sin He's still willing to let me into His kingdom one day." His jaw flexed as he turned to the window.

The thought of what a job like her uncle's required of the mind and body gave her pause. Would she ever be able to live up to that kind of standard? Was the pride in her heart enough to achieve her dreams of being more?

"God has a plan for you as well, dear. You need to start leaning on Him to figure out what that could be."

"In all the plans I've made, God led me there but never followed through."

"Those were your plans, not His. Remember that."

Pain welled in her chest, along with thoughts of what could've been with a life in the service, a life with Daniel. A happiness that disappeared all too quickly.

God, what's the plan now?

9

———————

Friday

The ringing phone woke Kenton, and he sat up straight. "Matthews."

"Well, I've got nothing."

"Bruno?" He frowned and looked at the clock. It was a little after six. "What're you doing up so early?"

"I finished the scans of the computers from the new employees. I wanted to make sure nothing else was tampered with."

He yawned and swung his legs to the floor. "You there already?"

"Yeah, Drone said I could come in early."

Rubbing his hand across his chin, Kenton frowned. "So, let me get this straight. You called me at six twenty to tell me you've got nothing?"

"Well, I mean, I figured you would want to know. After all, this case seems personal."

"It is, but call when you actually have information," he muttered as he stood, stretching out his back.

"You feeling okay?"

He ignored Bruno's chuckle. "You staying there?"

"I'll be here whenever you decide to show. You want me to text you when Ollie comes in?"

He stilled. "No, why do you ask?"

"Please, man. I've been around you when you're interested in a woman. I saw the sparks flying last night. Tell me you don't want to see her."

"Bruno, it's much too early in the morning for games."

"Well, get up and get in here. We need to find the mole."

"Be there in an hour."

"You might want to shave that shadow off. There's a dress code here, you know."

Kenton hung up, dropping the phone on the bed.

Scrubbing a hand across his face, he sighed. The thought of seeing Olivia made him pause and take a moment to remember the little number she'd pulled on him. The niece of a spy who acted just like a spy.

Man, if he couldn't get his focus together, he would be in trouble.

After shaving, showering, and dressing, he took off and stopped at the drive-through for a coffee. As he pulled into the parking lot, he noticed Marcus's silver BMW parked in the front. His watch read seven fifteen, and he smiled. At least he would have something to do this morning instead of waiting around with Bruno.

Walking through the lobby, he was escorted up the elevator and to a small workroom where Bruno sat, computer in front of him and coffee in hand.

"Glad to see you could make it," Bruno said without looking up.

"What's all this?" He sat at the round table across from Bruno and sifted through the files stacked in the middle.

"I printed out all the information about the three people

that started that day. I figured you might want to interrogate them."

He sighed and looked through each employee's paperwork. "So, nothing really meant nothing. There's nothing connecting them other than starting the same day the company was hacked?"

"Right. I'm going through the video feeds to track each of their movements throughout the day, see if anything stands out. But so far, nada."

Kenton started on the first folder as Bruno cleared his throat. "So, how was dinner?"

"Fine."

"Anything interesting happen?"

"No."

Bruno chuckled. "Surely there was something. Ollie is beautiful. You can't deny that."

"You didn't ask me that."

"Kenton."

"Bruno, this is a case. One we need to close, seeing how it's Friday. We've only got a couple of days to get this figured out and find a connection to Rashid. We don't get evidence, we can't convict."

Bruno sat up with a glare. "You know a pro like Halil Rashid doesn't leave proof or loose ends. There's not going to be anything to link him, so you may as well not worry about that right now. If one of these three did the hack, they won't know who it was for, and if they do, they won't give him up. He has a rep."

"So does Marcus."

A text alert made him pull his phone free from his belt.

Meet in my office in five. Got a line.

"Marcus has something. You gonna stay here?" He stood with coffee in hand, shoving the folders under his arm.

"Yeah, I'm still sifting through video. Is Ollie here yet?"

He shrugged. Bruno's smile grew.

"What?"

"Just admit you want to see her."

He chuckled. "Let's see, sit here with you or be in a room with Olivia? Hmm, not much of a competition."

"I see right through you." Bruno called out as Kenton turned and made his way out of the room and down the hall.

Pacing in Marcus's office, nervousness made his stomach clench. The thought of seeing Olivia was at the forefront of his mind, and he hated it. His focus should be on the threat, not her.

Well, it shouldn't be her.

"Sorry to keep you waiting." Marcus entered alone, slamming the door shut behind him.

"Everything okay?"

Marcus shook his head, yanking out his desk chair and sitting. He turned the monitor and motioned Kenton over.

An email sat on the screen.

You have my attention, Moore. I'm very curious who your help is, although I have a feeling I know. After all these years, I'm looking forward to seeing how this new development changes our game.

"I'm sorry, Kenton. I should've considered the effects of Rashid finding out you were helping me."

Kenton shook his head and stepped back. "No need. I've not been in hiding. If he wanted me, he could've tried to find me long ago."

"But I didn't want you in danger."

He chuckled. "You know that's not the way things work. We made enemies for life."

Marcus nodded. "I received this first thing this morning. It took a while to decrypt it. Our IT guys have been working to locate the IP address, but it bounces from one country to the next."

"You won't find him that way. You know that."

"Well, prepare for the attack it is, then. Your partner finished up the search of the computers early this morning and didn't find anything on the men and woman we hired the day of the breach."

Kenton nodded, holding up the folders from Bruno and walking back around the desk. "I want to interview them."

"I thought you might," Marcus smirked. "I put them in separate rooms alone and without access once they arrived."

Kenton followed Marcus out of the office and down the long hallway.

"Did you give access to a lawyer?"

Marcus shook his head. "Not necessary. They signed a disclosure when we hired them. We can question them without access to a lawyer as long as we have probable cause. Legally, they've given up their rights. Of course, they don't have to answer any questions if they don't want to, but that would terminate their job instantly. It also wouldn't look good when they apply for other jobs in tech."

Pausing outside the door, Marcus took the folder from the attached box.

"This is Marquis Layton. He's a data transcriber."

Kenton nodded and studied the information on the man. "I need Bruno here. He speaks the same language."

Marcus chuckled and pulled out his phone. "Please send Detective Price to the third-floor entry." He hung up and pocketed the phone. "He'll be here shortly. Now, I need to go discuss the situation with my security team."

He nodded as Marcus walked down the hallway, disappearing into one of the tech rooms. The elevator caught his attention as Bruno exited.

"What's going on now?"

"I need your help in the interview." He handed his partner the file, and Bruno smirked.

"You don't think you can speak geek?"

"Not in my wheelhouse."

"What is in your wheelhouse?"

He smiled and shook his head. "Nothing we're going to hear in this building, I assure you."

10

―――――

Olivia rotated her head, feeling the pop in her neck as she paced the security room during Marcus's briefing.

"So, we are to stay alert, and whatever the detectives ask for, they will receive it. Understood?"

Everyone nodded and then dispersed as Marcus fixed his gaze on her. "You all right?"

She sighed. "Just tired."

"Did you sleep last night?"

"Briefly."

Marcus took her hand. "Ollie, if you would like to take the day—"

"Are you suggesting that I, as head of your security, should take a day off when we have been threatened? If so, you are mistaken."

He nodded.

"What are the detectives working on?"

"Kenton and Mr. Price are interviewing the three employees who started the day of the hack. Mr. Price suspects one might've been responsible."

"And Kenton does not?"

Marcus grinned. "Kenton doesn't make those kinds of assumptions until he's reviewed all the facts. Although he's a man who will react when provoked, he takes his time and thinks things through."

"Okay, what does that have to do with the possible attack on Sunday evening?"

"Just information to think on, love." He squeezed her hand. "I'm going to go and see if I can calm the benefactors. Ever since that email and this new one—"

"New one? You didn't mention that in the meeting. What did it say?"

Marcus's eyes flashed dark as his jaw twitched. "I think I might have made a mistake asking Kenton to assist. Rashid knows he's the one who saved you. He's now a target."

"And how does Kenton feel about that?"

"He said he's not been in hiding, and he's more than capable of keeping himself safe." He nudged her side. "Although, I am more concerned about you being a target once more."

"Marcus. I'm taking every precaution, and I won't be taken by surprise again."

He nodded. "I've considered a bodyguard to keep up with you while outside the building."

"No. That's not necessary. You know it's not."

He sighed. "Rashid is evil. He will stop at nothing once he determines what he wants. If he wants you, Kenton is the only other person on earth I trust to keep you safe. If no bodyguard, please follow his lead until we're certain you are no longer in the crosshairs. Agreed?"

She licked her lips to reply, but Marcus rushed out of the room before she could form a sentence.

"You have got to be kidding me," she muttered.

Hearing Marcus say he didn't even trust her to keep herself safe was a heavy blow to her pride. She'd trained with men in hand-to-hand and done well advancing in her training. Not that she was impervious to a larger, stronger man, but ...

Staring at the screens in the security room, Kenton appeared off the elevators and headed for the room he and Detective Price were using as a workroom.

True, the man had proved himself a capable soldier. Coming to her aid, it was more than impressive. But allow him to be her bodyguard? Surely Marcus was joking.

Now aware of the danger, she was confident no one would surprise her like they had yesterday.

Kenton Matthews. With those piercing blue eyes, deep voice, and killer smile, why was he unattached? Their cat-and-mouse last night was more than enjoyable, and his willingness to play along was intriguing.

After being in the city for a year, learning this new job had taken up so much of her time that dating or relationships hadn't been an issue. Even here at work, there was rarely anyone to speak with on a personal level. It was nice to feel so comfortable with him.

Letting out a breath, she shrugged off the attraction.

"You have a job to do, and Kenton Matthews is only someone working alongside you. Get over it."

There was no reason to think about anything more or let the attraction build. Next Thursday, in less than a week, she'd be on an early flight to the UK to move on with her life. No more backtracking and no more loose ends that left her flailing.

Lord, please keep me on the right track this time. Don't let me lose sight of my path!

AFTER SPENDING several hours interviewing all three suspects, Kenton sat in the small break room serving as an office. Leaning back in the chair, he looked over one of the folders.

Alonso Downing caught his eye. The other two seemed not only disturbed by the breach, but their body language told him they were astonished to be considered suspects. Alonso, however, was angered, almost enraged at the accusation.

The door opened, and Kenton smiled as Olivia walked into the room. Slim jeans that cut her figure sveltely and a white button-up shirt that fit nicely made him peruse her from head to toe as she sat across from him.

"Subtle, Kenton."

He chuckled as she sat on the table. "Just returning the favor from last night, Olivia."

"I go by Ollie." She frowned.

"I know." He grinned as she let out a huff.

"I heard you interviewed a few of our people."

He nodded.

"Find anything?"

He picked up Downing's file and handed it to her. "Tell me what you think about him."

She took the folder and leaned back, reading over the pages. "He seems to have some anger issues."

"He was upset about being named a suspect. That seemed to supersede his need to prove his innocence."

She nodded. Setting the folder down on the table, she leaned over, her finger running across her bottom lip. As enticing as it was to watch her, he worked to push his attention elsewhere. She was much too good at stealing his focus.

"So, the reference is iffy at best." She frowned and flipped through the pages. "I want to talk to HR about him, find out who interviewed him and recommended his hiring."

"He might not be our guy."

She shrugged. "Either way, his obvious anger isn't an attitude I want at this company."

"I'll join you." Kenton stood as she pushed her chair back

and tucked the folder under her arm. He opened the door for her, and she smirked as she passed.

"Something humorous?" He caught up.

"No, just finding your gentlemanly habits interesting."

"Interesting? Because I opened the door for you?"

"Not just that," she said as they moved into the elevator, and she punched the button.

Leaning against the back wall, he smiled at the silence. She was good at keeping herself from engaging him, letting the tension settle.

"You know, you covered those bruises well."

"Takes a lot of makeup. Just feels sore."

"I can understand that."

She chuckled, turning to look at him over her shoulder. "I'm sure you can."

Following her out of the elevator and down the hallway, he paused when they reached another glass door. Inputting a numbered key and then swiping the card hanging off her wrist, they went inside.

"Josie, I need to speak with Martin." She scanned the folder and then closed it again.

"Yes, ma'am." The woman at the desk got on the phone as they waited.

***

Leaning against the desk, Olivia watched Kenton pace, his eyes securing every aspect of the room. She smiled at the action. This man was so familiar ...

"Ollie? What do you need?" Martin appeared around the corner, a huge smile on his face.

"Let's talk in your office."

Pushing past him, she set her jaw. When she first started last year, Martin was one of a few who decided they were much more intimate than coworkers. It was an attitude she'd had to put in check more than once.

Stepping into Martin's office, she sat down.

"Ollie, you know I'm free to speak anytime. But this seems unnecessary."

Martin put his hands on his hips and glared at Kenton from behind his desk. Kenton smirked in amusement.

"We need to speak to you about Alonso Downing."

Martin nodded, then sat down, his chair angled to her as he ignored Kenton. "All right, what about him?"

"Why did you hire him?"

Martin frowned as Kenton phrased the question.

"Ollie?"

"Why aren't you answering?" She leaned forward. "We need information about this man and why you hired him. Why won't you answer Detective Matthews's question?"

"I hired him because he is an excellent coder. His references are complete. I checked them myself."

"They are complete, but not what I would say shining." She leaned back and crossed her legs.

His leering pricked her skin. That was why she didn't wear skirts to work anymore.

"Martin, man, you're treading water here."

She held her fingers over her lips to cover her chuckle as Martin's gaze moved to Kenton.

"What's the problem?" Martin asked.

"He has anger issues. When questioned, he made it clear this company didn't hire him just to fire him a few days later, and he was adamant the legality of the situation was not transparent. We now have leaked information, an angered coder, and a threat against our facility. Want to ask any more questions?" She glared as Martin paled.

"I was not informed of his anger issues."

"Hmmf."

She frowned at Kenton's not-so-subtle reaction.

"I know the company he came from. They have excellent credentials and—"

"Yes, normally they do. But according to the paperwork, he does not. He was fired from his job, not laid off or let go or looking for a new, more challenging career. Why did you hire him?"

Martin turned red. "I'll send you the email I received about his skills. That's all I'm willing to discuss with the security officer and a detective."

"That's all you're willing to discuss?" she gritted out. "Let me remind you that this inquisition could very well start with this man who came to work here because of you and could be a possible leak and inside threat. If you value your job, you should tell us everything right now."

Martin turned a brighter shade of red. His jaw set as he glared and shook his head. She stood and placed a heavy hand on his desk.

"Of all the things you could do to destroy your career, this tops it. If we discover Downing is responsible for the breach of our system, not only will we prosecute him, but I will make it my priority to ruin you as well."

She stomped out of the room, barely containing her ire as she left the HR department with a slam of the door.

"Hey, wait up."

She punched the elevator button and clenched her fists, ignoring Kenton's voice.

"Easy, no need to bruise your hand too. He doesn't deserve that much attention."

Kenton followed her into the elevator, letting her have space and silence. Closing her eyes, she did her best to rein in her irritation.

As the doors opened, his hand moved across her back and pulled her out. She followed his direction to the break room, entering as he opened the door. She slammed the folder down on the table.

"I don't appreciate being talked down to or treated as if my opinion or my station isn't important."

He nodded, shoving his hands in his pockets.

"Martin is such a weasel." She moved to the fridge, pulling out a canned drink.

His chuckle made her pause. "Something amusing?"

He shrugged. "Actually, I was wondering if you two had dated, and that's why he was looking at you like that."

"No, never. It's taken all but a hit to the head to get it through to him."

She sat down at the table, flushed, irritated, and sore.

"So, that was a dead end. Even if we try another interview with Downing, I doubt we'll get anything different."

"Agreed. I'll see if I can get Martin in a room, go over all this once more with Marcus's permission."

"Really? That I'd like to see."

"So, we're back to finding the hacker." She frowned as he intently watched her from his spot, a smile building on his face. "What is it?"

He shrugged.

"You seem to have much more on your mind." Holding her chin in her hand, she studied his impressive smile.

He sighed and sat down. "Tell me something, Olivia."

"Ollie."

He grinned. "Why aren't you married and living it up in the UK?"

She sat back, crossing her arms and trying to control her surprise. "What? Why do you ask?"

He leaned in, those cobalt blue eyes shining. "You're an intelligent, capable, beautiful woman who has probably turned down her share of suitors. I'm just wondering why?"

"I ... I don't have suitors."

"I don't believe that."

"I don't. Back home, I trained a lot, focused on what I wanted to do with my life." She bit her lip a moment before letting it go. "I never had time for the one thing that would ruin everything I had worked for."

"What was that?" His eyebrow went up as his voice softened.

"A life much different than this one."

"Then why choose this one?"

She paused. "It was chosen for me."

He sat back, narrowing his focus, and she did her best to hold back any additional commentary or tics. Men like Kenton were apt at reading body language, and the mere fact he was studying her was ... well, almost intimidating.

This conversation was moving into a more personal one, and she was determined to keep from hashing out intimate details she had never divulged to anyone. Although, if it had to be someone, she assumed the man Marcus held in the highest esteem would be the best choice.

"You know, you purse your lips when you're thinking."

"You furrow your eyebrows," she retorted.

He cracked a smile. "Mind telling me what you were thinking about just then?"

She shook her head, then stood, moving to the window and leaning against the sill. Pulling out her phone, she did her best to appear busy, working to slow her heart rate despite the handsome and flattering Kenton Matthews staring once more.

11

"So, what's the plan for lunch?" Kenton leaned back in his chair as Olivia checked her phone.

"I haven't thought about it." She trailed off and he smirked.

Pulling out his phone, he called Bruno.

"Hey, find something interesting?"

"Let's go get lunch. Meet us downstairs."

"Us?"

He chuckled and hung up, then stood and stepped in front of her. "Come on. My treat."

She smiled. "Oh?"

With a grin, he took her elbow, easing her toward the door. "So, where's the best place to eat around here?"

"Depends on what you want."

He escorted her down the hall and to her office. Standing at the door, he waited for her to check her computer before grabbing her purse and coming back to meet him.

Another silent elevator ride later, they found Bruno waiting in the lobby.

As they exited the building, Kenton took Olivia's elbow

once more. "Just as a precaution, stay close, between me and the building."

She chuckled, then narrowed her eyes as she paused. "Kenton."

"It's my job while out here." He tensed his jaw as she nodded, pushing her purse strap higher on her shoulder.

Much debate over where to eat ended in a draw, so they settled for the American Burger down the street. Walking a block in the warmth of Dallas in October, he took a refreshing breath when they stepped into the air conditioning.

"This way." The waitress grinned and led them to a table.

"Can we sit away from the window, please?"

She nodded and moved them to a secluded table at the back of the room.

Guiding Olivia's arm, Kenton led her to the inside chair against the wall, facing the door. He took the seat next to her, and Bruno pulled out the chair across from her.

After ordering drinks, he opened the menu and immediately decided what he wanted.

Bruno studied the pages as Kenton leaned into the table. "Did you find anything on the video?"

"Give me a sec."

Glancing at Olivia, he watched as she pulled her hair up on top of her head and clipped it, tendrils falling against her face and neck as she perused the menu. With her hair up, it was hard not to notice her slender neck and the delicate chain that hung around it.

"So."

He turned his attention back to a smiling Bruno.

"I have yet to finish up the video of all the new employees. Did either of you find something interesting?"

He rotated his head, popping his neck as he rolled his shoulders. "You remember Alonzo Downing?"

Bruno nodded. "Yeah, he wasn't happy."

"More like angered."

"I remember him lashing out." Bruno's phone rang as he held up a finger and answered. "Price."

Kenton's gaze went back to Olivia, who was resting her chin in her hand. "You good?"

She cut her eyes to him and straightened. "Yes, just a lot on my mind."

"Maybe you should've stayed and taken a nap instead."

"I slept very well last night, thank you." She took a sip of her water and sat back in the chair, crossing her arms with a sigh.

"Be there in a minute." Bruno stood. "Got to get back. One of the guys helping me has made a mess of things. You good here? Or do you need a stretcher, old man?" Bruno's smile cranked up a notch when Olivia chuckled.

"Old man?"

Kenton ignored her comment and glared up at Bruno. "I think you can leave."

Bruno slapped his shoulder and headed out the door, brushing past the waitress.

After placing their orders, he turned to a smiling Olivia.

"Why 'old man?'"

"You seemed to think the same thing when we met."

She laughed. "No, I told you that I thought you would be much older based on the stories."

Her smile, her laugh, made her light up.

"I believe your first comment was, 'I thought you would be younger.'"

She smirked. "Coming out of the stressful situation I was in, you'll just have to give me that one." She took another sip of her water. "Besides, I saw the video of you entering the house."

He shrugged. "So?"

"How did you get over the brick wall?"

"Skill."

As she smiled, her eyes lit up. Man, he could get used to that smile.

"Exactly. Not too many people can do that."

"Are you trying to make me feel better about getting older?"

"I wouldn't call thirty-eight old."

He took a drink. "It's not. But with the job I used to do, the damage done, and the years of that kind of work, my body doesn't bounce back like it used to. The endurance I once had is long gone."

She searched his eyes before turning away, crossing her arms and setting her jaw. There was a lot on her mind today.

"What's got you thinking so hard, Olivia?"

"I go by Ollie."

He grinned. Her bright green eyes focused on his as her eyebrow rose.

"You do it just to annoy me?"

He shrugged and finished his drink. "Downing. If he is a contact, I doubt he knows for whom he works. It could be he's a scapegoat." Her eyes darted around the crowd in front of them. "I'm still running a program to find all the employees who were online at the specific time of the attack. Most were working on their programs or other work-related items. There were a handful not doing work-related tasks. I hope to uncover those and see if I can link someone to the attack."

"They would have to be online?"

She locked eyes with him. "No, not necessarily. But the other algorithm I tried to run failed, and I have a feeling it would be better for what we need. The hack could've come from a device such as a USB drive. If someone opened one up to see what was on it, that could be where the link was made, and they would never have realized what happened. But to send the information, the hacker would have to be online."

"So, you could determine what computers were working off a drive at the time of the attack?"

With a nod, her gaze searched ahead of her once again. "That was the goal, but it didn't work."

"Have Bruno take a shot at it."

"I'll talk to him when we return. If he has time."

"That's why we're here. He'll have time."

The waitress set down their orders along with refills, and he waited until Olivia placed the napkin in her lap before taking up her hand and bowing his head. "Lord, give us strength and patience as we fight against evil. Use this food to carry out Your will, and let our fight for justice not be in vain. Amen."

He heard a faint "amen" as he squeezed her fingers, then released them. Sawing into the large bacon cheeseburger, he took a bite.

"You know, if you're worried about your body and your age, maybe you should start eating better."

Wiping his mouth, he finished chewing and swallowed. "This is good for you."

She shook her head. "All that fat and grease."

"I'll work it off." He winked as she chuckled.

They ate in silence as he kept his eyes on the crowd milling around the restaurant. His gaze lingered through the window. A white SUV with tinted windows sat on the opposite side of the street.

He had already taken notice of the cars that were there when they sat down, and this one was new. The spacing looked odd, like the SUV parked between two parking spots, making it impossible for anyone else to fit.

Keeping an eye on the car, he finished his drink and set it aside.

Turning to Olivia, he tugged on her elbow. "Stay here."

Her eyes narrowed, and he saw that fight from yesterday lingering.

"Olivia, please stay here. I need to check something, and I don't want them spooked or leaving. I'll be right back."

She frowned but nodded as he stood, hurrying to the back of the restaurant.

Flashing his badge, he pushed through the kitchen and to the back doors. Instead of going to the street, he turned left out of the alley, jogging past the next building and up the next alley to cross the street. Coming up behind the SUV, he used the light on his cell phone and shined it through the back window.

Although still hard to see inside, it was enough for him to notice a canister sitting in the back, a few dozen wires hanging off.

He rushed back to the alley that sat far behind the SUV and called Bruno.

"Hey, man."

"Get a bomb squad here now. There's an SUV rigged to blow outside the diner."

"On it."

He hung up and groaned to see Olivia heading his way from the same direction he'd come. "I told you to wait."

"You didn't think I would see you out here?"

"You're the target," he gritted. "You need to go."

She scoffed and hung her hands on her hips. "Fat chance."

He shook his head as his phone rang. "Yeah?"

"This is Billings with the bomb squad. What've you got?"

"Possible bomb in an SUV. Windows are tinted, hard to make out, but there's a large canister in the back, visible wires hanging off. It's parked in an odd spot, not within the parameters or a normal parking job."

"That's it? A canister in the back? No actual threat?"

He bit back a comment. "Look, it's a real threat."

"I'll send a few guys to take a look."

"We need more than a few guys."

An annoyed scoff sounded. "If you don't have a verbal threat and can't even clearly see what's inside, how do you know what it is?"

"Experience." He hung up and barely kept himself from throwing the phone. "Idiot," he mumbled.

"They won't come?"

He shook his head. "Only sending a few guys, thinks it could be a hoax and waste of his time."

"But you're sure what you saw?"

He glanced at the stern expression on her face. "I'm sure."

She rolled her eyes. "Just ... sorry. I understand. You've got a point of view most do not."

He nodded, taking her elbow and moving her between him and the building with a frown. "Once the bomb squad gets here, the problem will be keeping them from blowing themselves up."

Glancing around the corner at the SUV, he wondered how he was going to get a good look inside the vehicle without triggering the device. If someone was watching, the bomber could detonate the second they approached.

His phone rang again. "Yeah?"

"Hey, where are you?"

He frowned and searched the road but didn't see Bruno. "Where are you?"

"I've got a drone flying above the restaurant. It's got amazing picture quality."

"Do you have infrared on that?"

"Yeah, man. It's got everything."

"Fly it over the white SUV on the road across from the diner. Switch to infrared and take some shots. The bomb squad isn't too interested and thinks it's not worth investigating."

"On it."

He hung up and watched the sky.

"What's going on?"

"Somehow, Bruno got access to a drone. It's got infrared capabilities, and if he can get a picture—"

"You'll have enough to get the bomb squad's attention."

He nodded. "I don't see or hear it."

"It's silent. One of the newest technologies we're developing." She stepped away from him, shielding her eyes as she looked up.

A few moments later, his phone rang again. "Yeah?"

"Got the pics. You're not going to like this."

"Why not?"

"Man, it's packed. Scans show a large container, and according to the data points, the images suggest all the doors are connected."

"Send them to the bomb squad now."

"On it. Stay back, man. This thing blows, no telling what's going to come out."

"Got it. When you get done with the pics, start scanning traffic cams."

"Already got them pulled up."

He leaned back against the wall as Bruno hung up.

"I'm guessing that was bad news."

His eyes locked on hers. "Large mass in the back. All doors are connected to each other. No way to tell if it's remote or on a timer or what."

Her eyes widened. "Then we need to start clearing people out."

"Wait for the bomb squad. We don't have authority here, and no one will listen. It'll just get the terrorists' attention."

She bit her bottom lip as she crossed her arms. "I'm not good at sitting around."

He chuckled. "Patience is one thing I can do. I'll have Bruno come get you so you can go back to the Institute."

"Not on your life. I don't like to be dismissed."

Pulling her to him and shifting her against the building once again, he gently rubbed her arms. "I'm not dismissing you. I'm trying to keep you safe. You know, that job of mine you keep forgetting about."

"Now, look. I've already pushed off the bodyguard Marcus was determined to hire, so don't you go making trouble too. Your job is to determine who's behind the hack and try to stop the next one, not protect me."

He grinned. "It's the same job now. And Marcus would agree."

With her heels on, she was practically eye-to-eye with him, her jaw tight as she glared. But with those amazing green eyes of hers, all he could do was smile.

"What's that grin for? You've not won anything."

"I wasn't thinking that." He raised his eyebrow, and a smirk teased at her deep red lips.

"Funny, Kenton."

He shrugged, looking over her face, enjoying the feeling of her being so close. "If you say so."

The echoing wail of sirens made him groan. "You've got to be kidding me."

A large van appeared and parked across the street as another parked up the street. Police officers descended on the area and started clearing patrons to safety.

"Well, I guess we'll get to see if it's remote-triggered."

Keeping a hand on Olivia's waist, he watched the officers move through the crowd and the bomb squad descending on the SUV.

His phone rang.

"Matthews." He frowned.

"Where are you?" Billings sounded irritated.

"A safe distance away. You, however, are not, and I guess we know now that the bomb is on a timer. You guys sure know how to make an entrance."

"Look, we do things by the book."

"After that entrance, if the bomber wants to, he can kill several officers and bomb squad members. You should've moved in quieter."

A deep sigh came over the line. "What do you suggest?"

"Nothing now. You guys have already done the damage. Just don't open that SUV by any door or window, it'll blow."

"We've got that, *detective*. Thanks."

He grunted, hanging up the phone and finding Olivia had pushed between him and the building to watch the chaos. Her body hugged his as she turned.

"Well, now what?"

He sighed. "We wait."

"Wait for what?"

"If they can successfully disarm it, we might get a lead on the bomber."

"But don't we already know who it is?"

"We do, but there's nothing to back it up. And I have a feeling there won't be anything to prove it with the bomb, either. Rashid does his own bomb-making and is very proud of what he creates. No signature, though. He's too smart for that."

"Then how do you ..."

He glanced down with a frown, and she nodded.

"Right, experience."

He chuckled. "But he is human and might make a mistake this time. Bruno is on the video from the traffic cameras, maybe he can get a picture. Even if it's grainy, a picture of Rashid or even something on the bomb, we'll be able go after him legally."

Armed with drills and protective shields, the bomb squad drilled into the back window, trying to make holes to insert pinhole cameras and get a look at the device.

After almost an hour, he tensed as a few of the men working on the SUV got too rough, and the vehicle started to shift.

"They're going to end up blowing it," he muttered.

Pulling out his phone, he took a few steps onto the sidewalk.

"Billings."

"Your men. You've got to calm them down. I can see the SUV moving."

"Matthews, we've got this."

"You don't understand." He took a few more steps, then noticed a flash within the cab. "It's going to blow!"

He took off, ignoring Olivia's voice. A sudden surge jerked him off his feet, and he flew backward, landing on the cement.

12

———————

His ears rang. Debris peppered his skin as Kenton let out a groan.

A hand gripped his arm, and he tensed as a body leaned into his. The smell of Olivia's perfume pushed his body back toward normalcy. Hands moved across his face, and he forced his eyes open to see Olivia kneeling over him, obviously calling his name.

He closed his eyes and, as he opened them again, pulled her hands to his chest. "I can't hear you."

The rattle in his throat proved he was speaking, but he couldn't hear himself. She continued to hover over him, withdrawing her hands from his and helping him sit up.

World spinning, he looked out at the chaos. The casualties would be limited to the personnel working the bomb, but that was still too much loss. His gaze moved to a man in a bomb vest, large and in charge and stepping into their space. He assumed this was Billings. At least he couldn't hear the man.

Olivia stood and went toe to toe with him. Judging by the red on Billings's face, they were arguing. He pushed himself to stand. The voices started to come through as he popped his ears.

"—warned you."

"He's a distraction at best."

Taking Olivia's hand, he pulled her behind him and pushed into the man's space.

"I'm Matthews. I told you what would happen, but you and your men didn't listen. This"—he motioned to the chaos—"This is on you."

Ignoring the man screaming at him, he pulled Olivia to the opposite sidewalk and back toward the Institute.

<hr>

TAKING LEAD, Olivia gripped Kenton's hand and led him toward the parking garage.

"I'm not leaving." His dry voice echoed in the structure.

"Yes, you are. You're bleeding and have no telling what all over your clothes." She frowned and held out her hand.

"No." He shook his head.

"Either yours or mine." She crossed her arms and waited.

His blue eyes searched hers as he pushed into her space. He was excellent at manipulating the situation, working to make her uncomfortable with his size.

"I'm driving. You need to sit."

Keeping herself from flinching as his cobalt blues stared into hers, she set her jaw. He finally pushed the keys into her hand with a grunt. She watched him walk to the large, black SUV at the end of the row, yanking open the car door and sliding inside.

Inputting the address into the GPS, she followed the directions and pulled up in the driveway of a beautiful craftsman-style home.

"Wait here." He slid from the seat, wavering a moment before standing. "Give me ten to clean up."

Ignoring her need to follow, she leaned back in the seat.

Watching him walk around the back of the house, she tried to ease the knots working their way up her neck after seeing him getting thrown. It had been terrifying.

After saving her life, she realized Kenton was much more than she had originally assumed. The legend Marcus had described seemed unreachable, unreal. But Kenton was very much flesh.

Having been around men like her uncle all her life, their habits and the way they studied and observed others were second nature. But with Kenton, there was just something different.

And all the acting as if she needed personal protection? She already had that from Marcus. She sure didn't need him acting all protective too.

She wasn't his job. Rashid was the one they should be focused on. The attack on her company's server, their cyberattack—that was the focus.

Shaking her head, she let out a deep breath.

"Yeah, the attack is supposed to be the focus."

Almost twenty minutes had passed, and she was tired of waiting. Sliding from the SUV, she went around back as she'd seen him do and stepped through the back door.

The house was silent, not even the sound of water running. Pulling her gun, she glided through the kitchen and living area, then quietly down the hallway. A few doors appeared and she frowned as she eased open the first door on her right.

A door opened, and she stilled. Kenton stood in the bathroom doorway, bare-chested, with a gun aimed at her.

"What—" He lowered his weapon as he held on to the doorframe.

"It's been twenty minutes. I was worried."

Ripping her gaze from his chest, she holstered her gun and stepped in close, frowning at the blood trailing down the side of his head.

A large cut sat above his ear. She moved some of the hair aside to see the damage.

"I'm fine," he mumbled.

She scoffed and used both hands to see the damage. "It's still bleeding and deep. You need it stitched."

"I'll do it later."

Unthinking, she slid her fingers through his messy and soaked hair to get a better look at the cut. He pulled her wrist down, shifting so she was right in front of him, her back to the doorframe. The woodsy aroma of his soap filled her senses as her other hand gripped his bare shoulder. They froze in space for a moment.

"Olivia, go wait in the car," he whispered as she kept her eyes from his, trying to focus on his chin.

His heavy breaths echoed in the silence as her heart pounded. He pushed her hand to his bare chest.

"Olivia."

"I should go," she muttered, wondering if he had heard her. Based on the fact he moved in closer, he wasn't listening.

"That ... would be best."

His breath warmed her forehead as she stared at his chest until he brushed past her, slamming the door and making her jump.

Closing her eyes, she exhaled and held her heated face.

Pushing from the doorframe, she rushed down the hallway and outside to the SUV. Once inside, she turned the engine on and kicked up the air conditioner as she leaned her elbow against the door and held her head. The sight of a bare-chested Kenton filled her mind, and that was an image she would not soon forget.

All the talk of him being old ... he had no idea. Muscular

and fit, he could probably out-press and outlift pretty much any man she knew. Then there were the scars. She'd seen similar marks on Marcus as well. They made her heart break.

Of course, Kenton's weren't as severe as her uncle's. But still, the slices stretched across his chest and stomach, the dark marks etched into his skin. She swallowed and focused on the house. He had suffered and she knew that, like Marcus, he would never discuss what had happened to him.

A knock on her window made her jump as Kenton pulled the door open.

"I'm driving." He took her elbow and pulled her gently from the seat, then led her around the front of the SUV and to the other side.

"Kenton."

He opened the door and waited until she sat down, pushing once more into her space. His blue eyes searched hers as his cologne filled the cab. "Yes?"

Staring at those eyes, trying to search the sudden mush of her mind, left her reeling. "Nothing."

Jaw tight, she pushed her focus to the front.

He waited a moment before closing her door. The drive back to the Institute was silent and tension-filled.

KENTON ESCORTED Olivia to her office, then headed to the one he and Bruno were using.

He was relieved to find it empty. He stalked the space and exhaled a heavy breath. Her standing there, pushing against his bare skin, had shifted everything.

Attraction wasn't an issue between them. But now, it would be much harder to walk away when this was all over. It had taken God's will to keep him from kissing her right then. Her fingers weaving through his hair, her hand gripping his shoulder and that perfume of hers engulfing his senses ...

He groaned and rotated his neck. The thing was, she was much more than a beautiful woman. His attraction was much more than physical, and it was taking all his energy to keep from doing something about it.

She was Marcus's niece, and although Marcus had already hinted at much more, there was no way Kenton could go down that path. His track record was terrible, and he was too old for her, too scarred. Besides, she deserved much more than a broken-down military man with commitment issues.

He couldn't allow her to become one of the women he hurt, disappointed.

He groaned.

God, what are you trying to do to me?

"Hey, you okay?"

He turned to see Bruno frowning.

"Yeah, no thanks to the bomb squad."

"You look good. You go home and change?"

He nodded and eased into the chair with a wince, pulling the files back up.

"Oh, so Ollie gave you a ride?"

"Drop it, Bruno. You got information for me?"

Bruno smirked and sat. "Well, it might not be anything."

"It's more than what we have now."

If Bruno was willing to sidestep the whole Olivia thing, it had to be something.

"I found video of your Downing guy talking to one of the other coders."

"So?"

"Well, it looked suspicious. Like they were trying to avoid everyone else."

"Did you background the other guy?"

Bruno nodded and stood. "Come on. I left my computer up and running in the other room."

He stood and followed Bruno out, walking down the corridor to the security office. Olivia straightened as they entered.

"I guess you already saw?" Bruno sat at the computer.

"Just explain it, man." He stepped in beside Olivia, lifting his arm and then dropping it before he placed his hand on her back.

"Fine. Here's the video. You tell me what you think."

He and Olivia leaned in to take a look. Downing was in deep conversation with another man, nervously checking over his shoulder, his head on a swivel. Their conversation stopped several times as people passed by.

"I think we need to have a conversation with that guy."

"That's Ray Coleston. He's head of the department. I find it hard to believe he was into something shady. He has a long history with this company and wouldn't give up any information. He's too clever."

"Then we need to outsmart him." He grinned at Olivia.

"She's right. I did some digging. The guy is a legend around here. He's developed more tech in his lifetime than most people even dream of."

Kenton leaned back against the wall, trying to get the smell of Olivia's perfume out of his mind. "So, he's had a long career. What would make him turn?"

Olivia sat on the edge of the desk as Bruno spun around to face him.

"You're thinking revenge?" Olivia smirked.

"I'm thinking credit."

He dropped his gaze from Olivia to Bruno. "How so?"

"Well, every design he comes up with belongs to the Institute. His ideas, everything he creates, are patented with the Institute, and he gets zero recognition. I mean, whenever they come out with something new, it's always 'the Institute has created this or that.' The actual designs, ideas, the men and women behind them, are never mentioned."

He nodded. "Makes sense."

"But why now? He's been here since the company began thirty years ago. He's had all the time in the world to find a way out. He could've simply moved out on his own, credited himself, and started a new company. With his credentials, he could have easily found financial backers." Olivia crossed her arms with a shake of her head. "The timing doesn't match. Besides, why would he trust Downing? The man's only been here a few days."

Kenton shrugged. "What if Coleston needed the money? We know Rashid is intelligent, too intelligent to simply ignore the tech coming from here. You said yourself it's a tech-lover's dream."

"Fantasy. I said fantasy."

Kenton frowned. "Either way, it might've taken time for Rashid to discover who he needed to target, to pull away from the firm and pay off."

"Can you hack into his financials?"

He grinned as Bruno rolled his eyes at Olivia's question.

"Of course I can, but it's not legal. There's not enough basis for a warrant, and although I won't get caught, I don't do illegal."

"How disappointing."

He covered his chuckle as Olivia stood.

"What about that other program you were talking about at lunch?"

She glanced up, her bright green eyes on his.

"What program?"

He ignored Bruno. "We need probable cause. If Bruno can help you with that program, we might get enough for a warrant."

"What program?" Bruno repeated as he sat up.

She sighed and turned to Bruno. "I wanted to create a program to determine who was online at the time of the hack and had access to a USB drive. The protocols I worked with didn't work. I mean, I couldn't get them to work."

"Let's see what you've got." Bruno grinned, and Kenton chuckled as Olivia sat, pulling up something on her screen.

As he watched the two work, he couldn't help but stare at Olivia. What was it going to take for him to forget about her? Because after this case was over, he would have to find a way back to his lonely existence, dating women who weren't right for him or would never understand him.

But Olivia would know, to an extent, who he had been.

His heart pounded at the thought of her standing outside the bathroom door, then running her hands through his hair. She had focused on his chest, the scars he had accumulated throughout his career. But she would understand and would never ask where they were from, how he got them.

As he hurried from the room, his jaw ached with tension. He needed a break from Olivia. On his way back to the workroom, his phone rang.

"Yeah?"

"I need to speak with you. Have you seen Ollie?" Marcus's clipped tone resounded over the speaker.

"Yes, she and Bruno are working on something, trying to link the hack to someone in the office."

"Then come alone. We'll fill her in later."

"On my way."

With a sigh, he hung up, hitting the button for the elevator. Focus, he needed that focus. Because if this all went badly, he would not only lose one of the closest friends he had ever known, he'd also lose much more.

Olivia was a target, and he was developing a fear for her, something he had never had for anyone else in his lifetime.

13

———————

Bruno had completed the algorithm, and the search was on. Olivia sat back to watch the screen, sifting through the data.

"It was an excellent idea. You just needed the right method." He gave her a wink.

She nodded, her mind drifting elsewhere. "How long have you and Kenton been partners?"

"About three years. After he retired from the Army, but I'm sure you already know all about him."

"Not really. Marcus only spoke of him here and there, a story on occasion." She fingered her lip, gazing at the door and wondering why Kenton left so suddenly when she and Bruno were getting started on a possible lead.

"I wasn't really talking about Marcus, you know. I have a feeling you do your homework." Bruno turned back to the screen.

"You think I'm playing spy, Detective Price?"

He chuckled. "No, but I think you like to play games."

She straightened as red crept up Bruno's neck. "What, exactly, does that mean?"

He shifted to face her. "Look, Kenton is a good friend. He's much smarter and more perceptive than he likes people to believe. He plays the good, strong soldier with little between his ears, but he's always a few steps ahead. Except when it comes to women."

She raised her eyebrow.

"Not like that." He chuckled. "He's too smart for some woman to string him along, wrap him around her finger. But he chooses to live a singular life, one I know for a fact he's decided he belongs to."

"And how do you know, for a fact?"

As much as she understood solitary men like her uncle, she also saw a handsome, dependable, worthy man when she looked at Kenton. He could have any woman he desired.

"He gets involved with women he knows aren't right for him. Gives himself an excuse to break up later. As intelligent as he is, I guess he's decided he'll never find someone he can fully be with." He frowned. "That's why, as a favor, I would appreciate you not playing some game with him."

She scoffed. "Game? What game am I playing?"

"Please, you have this whole mysterious, flirtatious spy game going on. I guess you learned it from your uncle."

She clenched her teeth. "I'd like to remind you that whatever you deciphered from our first encounter is to be kept confidential."

"I mean, I would never tell anyone ... I know you know." He let out a grunt as he turned crimson. "Look, he'd kill me for talking about him, so don't think I'm doing this for any other reason than I'm tired of seeing him deal with the wrong women. Just cut him some slack."

She stood, straightening out her blouse. "You must not think too highly of me, Detective Price, if you'd think I'd stoop so low as to deceive for gain."

He stood. "That's not what I meant."

"Kenton Matthews is a dear, dear friend of my only family. Marcus cares deeply for him, and I would never, ever do anything to damage that relationship. From what I've observed, Kenton could have any woman he wanted, if he actually wanted someone. Did you ever stop to think that perhaps he lives a solitary life because he knows no other?"

Bruno shook his head, crossing his arms.

"With this situation, dealing with a man determined to come after my uncle, a man from his past, don't you think Kenton's concerned about his past coming back as well? I'm not sure you're giving him enough credit." She frowned and headed out the door, squaring her shoulders and trying to calm her nerves.

It wasn't like she didn't feel the immediate attraction between them. But their coy game last night was all in fun. Taking advantage of him? That was off-limits with anyone so close to Marcus.

Standing in the women's locker room, she leaned against the wall and rubbed her forehead. The fact Bruno saw her as someone intent on getting what she wanted, no matter the stakes, was bothersome. Although, that was precisely the woman she'd trained to become.

"God, what are You trying to do?" she mumbled, straightening from the wall.

Everyone probably saw her as Bruno did—hard, unloving, and deceitful. Not the woman she was trying to be, much less what she wanted people to think. Those were the trappings of a spy, not a woman living in a self-imposed exile.

Is that Your plan? Show me how being a spy isn't worth the cost of losing my faith and the only family I have left?

Swallowing at the vindication that the world of espionage wasn't her calling, she let out a sigh. At least she'd be back in the UK with her friends next week. And if her interview went well, she would be back in the Army and finding her path once again.

Popping her neck, she frowned at the pain pulsing through her body and left the locker room to find her purse. She needed more pain medicine and a talk with Marcus.

"So, you think he's after her now?" Kenton looked up from the computer screen as Marcus nodded and began to pace.

The video showed a man with a laptop bag searching the lobby less than an hour ago. Then Marcus appeared, confronting the stranger and calling in the police. He finished the report, heart pounding at the thought of someone in the building watching Olivia.

"The threat is clear. Although this man won't reveal Rashid sent him, his job was to keep an eye on Ollie. He even had a picture of the rental she'd picked up this morning on his phone."

"I can take him in. See if he'll talk to me."

"No, it's being handled. The police are going to look through all his correspondence, try and find a connection."

"I'll call my boss. Ask him to check into it."

Marcus nodded as he sat against the edge of his desk.

"If he was already paid, we might be able to discover who deposited the money in his account."

"It's clear he has two targets now, Kenton. I can take care of Ollie, but the data, I'm afraid we're running out of time."

"Bruno has had some success and when I left, he and Olivia were working on a program to discover the hacker. If they can figure that out, we'll have a better grasp of what's going to happen and how. If we can get them to talk."

Marcus scoffed. "No one would dare admit to Rashid being the leader behind the mask. Even if they knew it was him."

"You're probably right." He collapsed in the chair across from Marcus.

"You feeling all right?"

Kenton's eyes snapped up to Marcus. "Yes, why?"

"That nasty cut is bleeding."

He frowned. Turning his phone on, he looked at himself in the camera. "It's fine."

"Tell me what happened downtown? Something about a bomb?" Marcus grinned.

He sighed. "The bomb squad and I had a disagreement."

"Oh?"

"That's another reason I didn't go federal. I don't want to have to explain every single thing to those who can't take my word for truth. I know what's going to happen because I've lived through most of it. Most people don't want to agree without proof."

Marcus nodded. "Understood. Do you think it was meant for you and Ollie?"

He shrugged. "Not sure. I think if it were, he would've detonated it when I moved in to take a look. It's the bomb squad's problem now."

He took the offered tissue from Marcus and pushed it up against his head. "Bruno and Olivia did find a person of interest, although Olivia is skeptical."

"Oh really? Who?"

"Ray Coleston."

Marcus frowned. "I agree with Ollie."

He chuckled.

"The man is an icon here, began with the company and has created nearly everything that's come through the department."

"We have him on video speaking with our angry coder, a man I've been looking at for the hack. They acted suspicious, and I want to have a talk with him."

Marcus crossed his arms with a sigh. "That's going to be tricky. He's got stake in the company."

"That's interesting."

Marcus nodded. "Not enough to make decisions, but enough to bail himself out should he end up in trouble."

"Marcus, I wanted to ask about this message. A man was arrested in the lobby?" Olivia entered, and Kenton gently pulled the tissue from his head, focusing on the bloody rag in his hand. "Why wasn't I informed?"

"I was in the lobby when it happened," Marcus said. "I found him. It's been handled."

"Why was he arrested?"

Kenton grimaced.

"He's a person of interest. The police will let me know why he was here and if there's anything to it."

"Marcus, if someone is arrested in the lobby, I'd like to know why. It is my job."

"I wouldn't dream of overriding your job. Kenton has agreed to look into it and keep us apprised."

An awkward silence stretched as he pulled out his phone.

"I suppose you already spoke to him about Coleston?"

He nodded.

Marcus cleared his throat. "He says you have reason to question him."

"Yes. The video of him and Downing is odd. The way they're acting, avoiding eye contact with others ..." When she trailed off, Kenton looked up to see her frowning down on him. "You're bleeding again."

"So I've been told."

She sighed. "Come to the table. You need stitches."

He frowned as she headed to a cabinet at the other end of the room.

"I can do it later."

"It'll be trailing down your head by then."

"Go on, Kenton. Or I can do it if you prefer."

He glared up at Marcus. "No thanks. Still have a nasty scar from the last time you stitched me up."

Olivia chuckled. "He doesn't do a very good job."

Kenton sighed and stood, striding to the chair and table as she searched through a red kit.

"I have some glue. Let's try that first."

Jaw tight, he allowed her to lean his head to the side, her fingers moving through his hair. With Marcus watching them, this wasn't as intimate as last time, but it still brought on a reaction as he gripped his hands together.

"This will sting."

The gel burned like fire as he sucked in a breath.

"Ollie, perhaps you should speak to Ray. Not an interview, of course, just a casual discussion." Marcus's voice resonated in the quiet office.

She sighed, a frown forming on her lips. "Not sure that will do any good."

"Worth a shot."

Her green eyes lit on his for a second before she pulled back, capping the lid to the gel and shuffling the kit around.

"I'll think it over."

Kenton's phone rang and he stood, pulling it from his pocket. "Yeah?"

"Come take a look at this." Bruno sounded more than excited.

"Yeah, on my way." Kenton hung up. "Bruno thinks he might have something."

"I need to speak with Ollie for a moment."

Kenton nodded to Marcus and headed to the door.

"Get a grip," he muttered to himself, punching through the stairwell door and descending to the floor below to see Bruno.

14

"What's on your mind, Ollie?"

Olivia sighed and sat, chucking her heels and pulling her legs onto the couch. "I told you earlier, I'm tired."

Marcus sat across from her with a frown. "Not exactly the answer I was looking for."

"What are you looking for, then?"

He chuckled. "There's something else bothering you. What is it?"

"Just a comment that struck me wrong. I suppose everyone around here sees me as some robot-like human, unable to relate to anyone."

Marcus scoffed. "That's what's wrong? Some idiot who can't have you decided to be hasty about his words?"

She smirked. "No, he's not an idiot, and he's not interested in me. I just ... he's not wrong. I don't do well with personal interactions."

Marcus leaned forward. "You have your reasons. And I, for one, am thankful I haven't had to take any action against some rube that decided to break your heart." He winked, and she chuckled.

"It's not that."

"Oh? Because that's exactly what it sounds like." Marcus took ahold of her hand. "Is this about Kenton?"

Her eyebrow went up. "Why, no. It's about me. My inabilities."

"Then what do you plan to do about it?"

"Perhaps when this is all over, and I'm back in the UK ..." she mumbled.

Marcus squeezed her fingers. "That's a conversation for later."

She nodded and eased to her left with a grimace.

"Are you alright?"

"Just the burn on my side."

"You need a doctor?"

"No."

His eyes narrowed as he frowned.

"Really. It's just sore."

"Fine. Now, about Coleston."

"I'll speak with him. But I doubt he'll give me anything. I've tried to talk to him, but he never has anything to say."

"I'm sure your conversation skills have improved since you last spoke."

With a sigh, she pushed her feet back into the heels and stood, squeezing Marcus's hand before letting go. "I'll let you know."

"No, we'll be watching."

Her face heated as Marcus stood. "We? Why do you need to watch?"

He shrugged. "Just a precaution. If he is involved, it could be dangerous for you. You've been through enough." He kissed her cheek, and she followed him through the door to the elevator.

"Send me the stills of him and Downing, just in case I need them."

Marcus nodded. "Keep your phone out, and we'll listen in.

Let me know if you need me." He winked as he exited the elevator, joining Kenton in the second-floor lobby.

She nodded and glanced at Kenton's blue eyes before the doors closed.

"Girl, get yourself together," she said as she hit the sixth-floor button.

The way she had acted with him, pushing his buttons and allowing him to do the same to her, was flirtatious. It didn't mean something more resided between them. The sooner she figured that out, the better.

Besides, moving back overseas should temper any lingering feelings, right?

As the doors opened, she sighed and stepped through, turning right toward Coleston's office. Time to find a way into his reserved space and get that focus back.

Knocking on the door, she took down her failed bun and hurriedly brushed her fingers through the strands of hair as he called to enter.

Opening the door, Coleston sat at his desk, his dark eyes narrowing as she entered.

"Miss Lloyd, what brings you to the sixth floor?" He stood and held out his hand.

She shook it with a nod. "I have a few questions about one of your team members."

He frowned. "Yes, Downing. I heard you interviewed him. Please have a seat."

She forced a smile and sat down, leaning to her right to ease the pain working up her left side. Setting the phone in her lap, she confirmed the Bluetooth link in the corner had connected. "I'm just here for a conversation, Ray. This isn't an interview. Nothing on record. I just want to know what you think of the man."

Coleston studied her for a moment, his lips pursed and hands clasped on top of his desk. "Downing is an intense worker. He sets high stakes for himself and works hard to make his goals."

"Have you known him to be irritated or upset?"

"Not that I can recall. Why?"

"He seemed more than a little upset when he was interviewed. The detective I spoke with said he was much too angry about why he was there instead of simply giving up the information asked of him."

Coleston flinched. "What information do you think he has?"

She shrugged, noting the man's strange reaction to her comment. "All the detective wanted to know was his daily schedule when he arrived on Monday. Downing refused to answer. It caused the detective to become more curious."

"Doesn't seem so suspicious to me. Like I said, he's an intense worker. I assume that attitude is just part of his character."

"The information we're looking for would help either confirm or deter our investigation. Does Downing have any access to anything protected?"

"No."

She frowned at his quick response. "And how do you know so definitively?"

"I know what everyone on my team is working on at all times. Right now, Downing is working with correction and recoding our measures on several older systems."

"Do you speak with him about anything other than work?"

Coleston shook his head.

"We can't find anyone who spends time with him here at the office. I wondered if you knew of anyone who might be able to give us more insight on his character."

"No one I can think of."

She nodded and stood, sliding the phone into her pocket. "Thanks for your input. I appreciate you speaking with me."

"Miss Lloyd?"

Pausing, she turned back to see him standing, his face red and his fists clenched at his sides.

"Are you certain this was simply a conversation?"

She nodded, crossing her arms and setting her stance. Angry and irritated, he resembled Downing's appearance during his interview.

"If you think someone heard us through your phone, you're mistaken. This room is locked down."

Her pulse kicked up a notch. "I don't need anyone to listen in on our conversation. I told you this was off the record."

"I've heard about you."

She tilted her head and permitted herself a smirk. This was something she could use to her advantage. "Oh? And what have you heard?"

"There's a reason you're here as head of security. You have more skills than you let on."

Taking a few steps back toward the desk, she hoped pushing the tension would get Coleston to slip.

"Just one more reason I don't need anyone to listen in on my conversation with you. I can handle myself just fine without anyone coming to rescue me." Leaning on the desk, she met the man's glare. "I've seen a few things about you that make me wonder, though."

Coleston's face went crimson.

"You seem awfully close to Downing. Something you just denied. That makes me wonder exactly what you're hiding." She tilted her head as she tapped the desk.

He was holding back, maybe another push ...

Taking out her phone, she pulled up the pictures and showed them to Coleston.

"You see, this entire conversation was taped, and as people pass by, you stop talking until they're out of earshot. Now, the camera doesn't give us the verbal cues, but I do think if I took the time, I could read your lips." She grinned as the man's eyes dropped to the phone and then glared back at her.

"I can't believe you would accuse me of threatening this company. I helped to build this company, and I have enough at stake to destroy you." His words came out bitter and heated.

She shrugged. "I'm not concerned about my job if that's what you're implying. If you're speaking about a more physical attack, I would think twice." She leaned in, studying the man who looked like his blood pressure was about to make him collapse. "I would think long and hard about that kind of destruction."

Turning, she opened the door and stepped into the hallway, pausing at the sight of Kenton standing outside the elevator, his gun to his side.

She sighed and made her way to the open elevator. The sound of his weapon being holstered followed behind her as she hit the third-floor button.

"What happened in there? We lost audio and video."

"The man has something going on. I think we might have a mole."

"What'd he give up?"

She ignored the fact he was staring as the doors opened. His hand pulled at her elbow to get her out of the elevator, and she paused, yanking away.

"He didn't say anything. He has a protective shield in his office, preventing outside interference. That by itself isn't enough to go on, but if we can get into his system, we might find a connection."

Kenton pushed into her space, making it impossible to avoid his gaze.

"Next time, you need to get out."

"This is my job."

"And my job is to protect you. I can't do that if I can't see or hear you."

She leaned in, clenching her jaw and seeing his set as well. "Your job is Rashid. Not me. Don't get confused about that. I don't like being handled, and you are pushing the bounds consistently."

His cobalt blues cut back and forth.

"Um, excuse me?" Marcus's voice sounded, and she narrowed her gaze before turning a glare on her uncle.

"I assume you're the one that sent him in?"

Marcus's red face was stern. "Ollie."

"No, I need to be taken seriously. Between Martin and his defiance, Kenton, and now you, why am I even here if you think me so inept? Leaving seems to be the right plan."

"You're not inept, and you know that. I'm worried. You don't know Rashid like we do." A muscle twitched in Marcus's jaw.

She had only seen Marcus upset a few times in her life, and from the stern expression on his face, she was pushing his buttons. It wasn't something she enjoyed.

"All right, then. Let's talk. I have a few ideas." She turned toward the security room, a breath on her lips and a lump in her throat.

Lord, what is Your plan here?

Because if her uncle felt she was so incapable of doing this job, how in the world could she make it in the military?

15

Trying to calm the fear and anger sweeping through his body, Kenton blew out a deep breath and rested his hands on his hips. It had taken all his energy to keep from storming out of the surveillance room when they'd lost the video and then the audio. Once Marcus nodded, Kenton had moved in, ready to take the door down if needed.

"I think we need to ease into this."

He glanced at Marcus, then turned his gaze on the office door Olivia had walked through.

"You said it yourself. She doesn't understand."

"Yes, but we've seen the worst of the worst. He's not here, not in this building, and we can protect her."

Kenton nodded and faced his friend. "I'll follow your lead. She's your niece. You know what she can handle."

Marcus chuckled. "I have a feeling my lead isn't going to matter. You two seem to have something."

"Marcus." He frowned as Marcus shrugged with a grin. "What did she mean leaving is the best idea?"

Marcus's grin dropped. "She's not happy here and plans to go back to Britain to re-up."

His heartbeat kicked back up. "She's already got a spot waiting?"

"She thinks with her credentials, her training, she'll be able to make a name for herself. I believe boredom is the term she used earlier." Marcus brushed past him to the office.

It was a disappointing thought. Her leaving after this was all over. But it did cap his worry about finding a way to disengage. If she left, moved across the ocean, he would be able to forget about her.

He sighed and followed Marcus into the room.

Marcus sat in the large chair. Olivia leaned against the desk edge, facing him. Kenton stood to the side of the door, shoving his hands in his pockets and trying to keep from staring at her.

"So, we're going to start with Martin?" Marcus leaned back in his chair.

"There was something about how he acted as I questioned him about Downing. He was uneasy."

"Could be the way you were glaring at him."

Olivia cut her eyes to Kenton for a millisecond as he smirked, then refocused on Marcus. "If you could speak with him, we'll follow that lead first, then go on to Coleston."

Marcus nodded. "I'll get it started."

"What did Bruno discover?" Olivia turned once again to him, frustration and exhaustion building behind her eyes.

"The new protocol you two worked on spit out a list of names. We started going through them. Between video and Bruno going through the systems, we should be able to narrow it down."

"Was Downing on the list?"

He glanced at Marcus. "No, but Coleston was."

Marcus nodded with a frown. "That is concerning. I'll bring it up with the board, but no one will consider Coleston unless we find something concrete. He's too important to this company."

"Bruno is still digging."

Marcus nodded, then turned his attention to Oliva. "Now, as far as housing tonight."

Olivia groaned, stood from her perch on the desk, and crossed her arms as she paced.

"You need to stay inside until I arrive. I'll update the board, and I don't know how long it will take." Marcus frowned, then glanced at Kenton. "Go ahead and take her home."

"What?"

Kenton straightened as Olivia turned red, her mouth agape as she stared at Marcus.

"Marcus."

"Either he takes you home, or I'll hire that protection detail to take you home and stay with you in the house." Marcus stood and took hold of her arms. "This is just so you can get some rest. You've been through the wringer the past two days. I'm just trying to make it a little easier, nothing against you."

She huffed. "You don't have to walk on eggshells. I get it."

Marcus kissed her forehead and released her arms. "Now, go gather your things. I have something to discuss with Kenton before you leave."

Olivia nodded and left the room, ignoring him completely.

As the door shut, Marcus grunted. "I'll send you directions to the safe house I've set up for the two of us."

"You want me to hang around until you get there?" Part of him wanted to be there for her, but the other part saw things going much differently than Marcus imagined if he stayed.

"I don't think it'll be an issue. This house is off the grid. There's no link to either of us, and we haven't been there in over a year. Just lose any tails."

"Not to worry."

His friend sighed and shook his head as he shoved his hands in his pockets. "I'd be lying if I said I wasn't more than a little concerned about her. Until Rashid is caught, we'll be a target wherever we go. Perhaps getting her away from me will help. If she still wants to go back after all this is over."

"Don't make any hasty decisions, Marcus. You once gave me that advice, and I'm giving it back. Think it through. Putting space between you doesn't change who she is, her habits, her friends, her routines. She stands out in a crowd."

Marcus nodded. "I agree. Thanks for the reminder."

Kenton chuckled and headed out the door to find Olivia.

16

———————

Olivia gathered her things from her office and headed to the door.

Kenton stood on the other side, his lips a straight line. "Let's go."

She complied, trying to balance appreciation for his need to help and irritation at the intrusion into her space as he led her to the elevator.

After another silent ride, his arm slid around her waist as he led her from the elevator and to the parking garage. He pulled her in, and the aroma of his cologne made her take a deep breath. Her mind was shot if she was allowing herself to feel so overwhelmed because he smelled so amazing. Maybe she was too tired and needed some rest.

She slid into the open SUV door. He shut it and moved to the driver's side, pushing in behind the wheel.

In silence, he took out his phone and scrolled through it before starting the SUV and backing out of the lot.

"Do you have babysitting duty?"

The muscle in his jaw jumped. "I'm not staying if that's what you're asking."

She turned in her seat to face him. "If anyone here is to be upset and irritated, it should be me. You sure wouldn't let me treat you the way you're treating me if the roles were reversed, would you?"

"This is different. You know that."

"Not so different. Besides, you forget I don't have to let any of you help me. I can lose a protection detail or even force you out of my house if necessary."

He chuckled. "Is that so?"

She did her best to stifle a smile, shaking her head that it took so little for him to change her mood.

"How about a peace offering? So you don't have to force me from your home."

She chuckled and leaned against the door, glad his stuffy mood was gone. His wide grin made his face light up, and her eyes wandered over his profile. She felt more than a little attraction rising again.

"Olivia?"

"Yes?"

"Peace offering."

"What is it, specifically, you're offering?" She leaned into the console, putting her chin in her hand to watch him.

"Your pick."

She grinned, already noticing the shift in his body since she leaned closer. At least now, she had no doubt the attraction ran as deep on his side. "How about that story of how you got the knife back?"

He glanced at her with a sigh. "That's ... tricky."

"Leave out what you need to. Surely you can give me the basics." She kicked off her heels and pulled her legs onto the seat. With the rush hour traffic, it would be a while before they reached the house on the city's outskirts.

His jaw shifted back and forth as his eyes checked the mirrors.

"I'm sure I can come up with something else. Perhaps when Marcus gave you stitches?"

"Same story," he murmured.

With a sigh, he settled into the seat as traffic came to a standstill. He looked over, his expression easing as he studied her. "I was called into a part of the world I was familiar with, a job lined up." He licked his lips. "My guys and I had to gain intel on a group. As we went in, we camped down for a day or two, gathering as much as we could. A name popped. Marcus." He glanced at her before going back to the mirrors.

"I told my guys to keep track of everything else. I was intent on finding out what they had and whether Marcus was in danger. It'd been a few years since I had seen him. We had talked a few times—over secure lines, of course. He always managed to get in touch with me." He shook his head with a grin.

"Anyway, I discovered he was a target. Our command told us to get out. We had stayed as long as we could, and I was the first one out. I wanted to get a message to Marcus as fast as possible. When I reported what I knew, my commander was privy to our previous situation and agreed I needed to contact him."

He cleared his throat. "He did some digging, found Marcus's location from a contact after he related what I heard. I took a plane ride and tracked him down. We used the same relay from our previous meet and he found me quickly. I told him what was going on, and we were attacked."

She sat up. "Did they follow you?"

He shook his head with a frown. "They had dug in before I arrived. He was escorting a man of prominence, and after my message, Marcus was smart enough to send the man away before meeting me. Their schedule had been the same for a week, so it wasn't hard to track where Marcus would be."

She scoffed. "Marcus is too careful about that. He would

change up routes, meeting places, everything. You know him. He doesn't do routine."

Kenton chuckled. "No, he doesn't. But he was no longer in the SAS. He wasn't a spy, he was protection detail. When we were attacked, he was livid. He had told his employer the risk of being so predictable, but no one thought anything of it. After all, the man he was protecting didn't have any enemies in that part of the world."

She nodded.

"God gave us a reprieve and allowed us the chance to escape. I had a gash across my back, and he had a head wound. We were bloody and beaten but alive. The rest of the detail he worked with got wind of what happened and sent in troops to take care of us. I kept low, out of sight. I wasn't exactly someone who could blend in, and no one knew who I was or why I was there.

"I holed up for a while and by the evening, Marcus came in with supplies. He stitched me up, bandaged me, and kept me fed until I was good enough to travel and get back home. It was a nasty cut, I can't see it well, but what I can see is pretty bad."

She frowned as he chuckled, upset by the way he seemed to see his life. "Kenton, the things you've been through, do you ... I mean, does it seem serious to you?"

He frowned. "Serious? Really?"

"The stories you tell, the danger you've been in, you tell them as if they're nothing. Marcus does the same thing."

His jaw tensed as silence spread.

"It's not that they're nothing. The things I've seen, done, been a part of, they're what my life in the service required of me. I came out alive, and that's not something I take lightly." He glanced at her. "Have you seen Marcus's chest?"

She swallowed with a nod, feeling heat on her face. "Once. He was changing. I thought it was some kind of tattoo at first, it was so big."

"The first time I met him, that's what Rashid had done to him."

She took a breath, her jaw dropping.

"Those things I can't unsee. I can't make it disappear from my mind. But I do look back on how we got out, the friendship we cemented, and smile. Because we survived. At the time, you don't know if you'll live or die. You fight, do what you can to make it out and protect your buddy. Then, if you live, you can look back and smile, seeing the good that came from it."

"What good?" she whispered.

He shrugged and pushed the car into park, turning to face her. "I survived, Marcus survived, and we found a friendship that has protected us for the past decade. It's not a common thing. So many don't make it, and many don't make a connection like we have. I consider myself lucky to have met Marcus Moore."

She nodded as he turned off the SUV and got out, leaving her sitting in the dimming lights of the car. Her door opened and she turned. Kenton stood in the space, taking hold of her hands.

"Olivia, when Marcus and I worry for you, it's because we know what the enemy is capable of. It's not you. It's not your lack of ability." He swallowed as his blue eyes searched hers. "I assumed Marcus never discussed what happened with Rashid to you. But that scar, I see it often." He leaned closer, squeezing her hands. "You understand now?"

She nodded and dropped her gaze, trying to keep herself in check as he pushed into her space.

"I'm sorry you had to go through so much," she said. "I'm glad you survived."

He chuckled, pulling strands of hair from her cheek, tracing his finger down her skin before dropping it. "Me too."

He stepped back, and she slid from the seat as he took hold of her waist again, leading her to the front door. She handed him the keys and he unlocked the door, dropping her waist to take out his gun.

As they stepped through to the entryway, he shut the door and turned to her.

"Stay here."

She nodded and leaned against the door, locking it and turning on the alarm. He stalked down the hallway, then up the stairs.

He descended the steps, holstering his weapon. "It's clear. Marcus should be here in a few hours."

She nodded again, unsure how to react after what he'd shared and their close proximity.

"Olivia?"

She smiled and looked into his blue eyes. "I'm fine. I'll see you tomorrow." Turning, she unlocked the door and hit the alarm button to silence it.

Kenton paused at the open door, facing her again. "If there's anything off, you call Marcus or me, okay?"

She nodded.

"Olivia, promise." He leaned forward, taking hold of her waist once again.

"I promise. I'll be fine."

The standoff continued as his eyes searched her face, dropping to her lips often. Taking a breath, she hugged his waist. He gripped her tightly, releasing a sigh and making her grin.

"Thank you for sharing with me. I promise not to bring it up with Marcus."

He chuckled, his fingers pulling at the ends of her hair. "I would appreciate that."

She pulled away, leaning against the door with a smile, enjoying the grin on his face.

"This isn't some trick, is it?"

She tilted her head to the side. "You think I'd try and trick you?"

He chuckled and tugged at the hem of her shirt. "I never know with you. You seem to have some kind of draw to you."

She straightened, a lump filling her throat. "Did you speak with Bruno?"

His brow furrowed. "No, why?"

Searching his eyes, he didn't appear to be lying.

"Why?"

"Just something he said."

"What did he say?" His voice dropped as he stepped closer.

"Don't worry about it." She dropped her gaze to his chest. "I just ... never mind." She pushed her palm to his chest, trying to back away.

"I trust you. Do you trust me?"

She snapped her eyes to his. "Why would you even ask?"

"You step back a lot. Why?"

She frowned. "That has nothing to do with trust."

His grin surfaced, and he leaned down, pressing his cheek to hers. "Just keeping up with you. You're good at getting people to open up, and I'm trying to do the same."

Kissing her on the cheek, he quickly retreated down the porch steps and to his SUV. She slammed the door and locked it, her jaw agape.

"What ... what just happened?" she muttered, her face on fire.

Setting the alarm, she shook her head and grabbed the phone from her purse. As exhausting as the day had been, she needed a workout, something to help her forget about the interactions with Kenton. He was too amazing, too smooth, and the way he seemed to look right through her ... she needed to get herself in check.

With a sigh, she pulled out some sweats. This was going to be a long night.

17

After working out for an hour, Olivia's exhausted body ached, but her mind spun. Her cheek was still on fire from Kenton's kiss.

That was just crazy, right?

After showering and checking the house and alarm, she decided it was definitely time for bed. If only her focus would agree. Working in such close contact with Kenton, dealing with his protective tendencies was going to get harder and harder.

At first annoying, she was starting to appreciate his protectiveness. Marcus had been the only one in her life who wanted that job. Now, Kenton was pushing that boundary all too often.

After his story this evening, she at least understood him and Marcus a little better when it came to Rashid. It made more sense now why they were so overprotective.

With a sigh, she rolled over and stilled. The quiet of the house made her frown. Something nagged at her mind as she sat up. That sixth sense Marcus had ingrained in her went off.

Grabbing her gun and phone from her nightstand, she quietly slid off the bed and tiptoed to the side of the armoire.

She dialed Marcus, but it went straight to voicemail. That was uncommon. He usually answered her calls.

The door sat on the other side of the large, antique armoire, and she stilled when a click sounded. The phone vibrated against her hip, and she put it to her ear.

"Someone's here." She barely whispered the words and hung up, shoving the phone back into the waistband of her leggings.

The door opened. She felt the change in air pressure and heard the muffled steps on the carpeted floor.

A gun appeared around the armoire, and she grabbed it, shooting the man in the side, hoping the armor would be slight. Pushing him down, she barely dodged the shot from a second teammate as she fired back with both weapons, then collapsed on her side as a third came into the room.

Twisting onto her arm, she took out the man's legs, then kicked his throat as he landed, her leg falling across at just the right space between his helmet and body armor. He gasped for air as she swung the butt of her gun around and hit the side of his head.

Rolling to stand, she rushed to the opposite side of the door, hiding behind it and waiting. There were only three here, but last time there were four.

Stilling, the subtle click of the front door and the footfalls on the steps lingered as she readied for another battle.

A large body stepped into the room, and she went to strike, biting back a yelp as the man's arms encompassed hers, pushing them up as he blocked her kick. She was swung around, and an arm went around her waist as he held the gun in her hand.

"It's me, Olivia," he hissed.

Kenton squeezed her back into his chest, and she took a breath and nodded, releasing the gun to him.

"You okay?" He pulled her around and lifted her chin. In

the dim moonlight filtering through the window, he frowned as his hand moved down her jaw and swept her hair off her shoulder.

"Yeah, fine. Did you see anyone? There are only three." She tried to step away as he dropped his eyes from her to the ground.

"They dead?"

"One should still be alive."

He squeezed her waist before he released her, clearing their weapons and checking each one.

"This one is alive." He pulled some zip ties from his back pocket and bound the man's wrists and ankles together. "I'll check the house. You stay here."

With a glare, he pulled the gun from his back and headed down the stairs. "And call the police."

She pulled out her phone as she collapsed on her bed.

"911, what's your emergency?"

"I'm at 2012 Devonshire. I just had three men come into my home. Two are dead, one unconscious. I have a friend here checking the rest of the property."

"Ma'am? Are you sure you're okay?"

"I'm fine. Please send the authorities."

She hung up and fell back on her bed, easing the adrenaline surge through her body.

"I think we're good."

She sat up and groaned as Kenton stood in the doorway with a smirk.

"What's that for?"

He shrugged. "Never seen you relaxed before. No power outfit, no heels."

"Yes, I'm sure that's the most important thing to notice here."

She sighed as he came closer, a frown darkening his face.

He pulled her arm up and pushed the sleeve to her shoulder as she winced.

"You got nicked." He swiftly moved to the bathroom, returning with a towel. He sat down next to her, wrapping the towel around her left arm with a grunt.

"It's just a cut. Nothing serious."

His jaw tightened as he lifted her arm to rest on his shoulder.

"Kenton."

He leaned in, making her pause as his blue eyes caught her attention. "That was too close. This was too close. You need someplace safer, and you need armed guards."

"You're kidding. You have no idea—"

"No, I don't know who trained you, and I realize you're trained well. But you can only handle so many attacks before the lack of sleep gets to you and you make a mistake. You're running on fumes here. I think you need to carefully reconsider what you need."

His soft voice made her skin prick with goosebumps, his eyes drifting to her mouth every so often and taking away her breath. As his fingers slid across her jaw, he rested his hand on her neck. He wouldn't push for something here, not after all this.

Sirens echoed downstairs, and the sound of the front door slamming to the wall severed the moment.

"Police! Anyone here?"

"I'll call Marcus." He slowly lowered her arm, once again pulling some hair from around her face before he stood.

Swallowing hard, she watched with wide eyes as he walked to the doorway.

"We're up here and unarmed. There are several weapons on the floor, though."

The police made their way upstairs, and the same detective

who had come to clean up after yesterday's attack appeared with a frown as he flipped on the light.

"Miss Lloyd. Here we are again."

"I'm glad you're here. This will go faster."

"Why are so many people trying to kill you, Miss Lloyd?"

She stood, bracing herself against the bed as dizziness overwhelmed her. "I work for one of the most advanced technological facilities in the world. We're dealing with a threat, and it seems the perpetrator is trying other ways to get what he wants."

The man sighed and shook his head as Kenton pushed past him and gripped her elbow.

"She's been nicked and needs medical attention. I'll drive her."

"And you are?"

Kenton pulled out his badge. "Detective Matthews. I'm working the threat at her company. Her uncle called me to check on her. This is what I found."

The detective looked between them and finally nodded. "Tell your uncle to call me immediately."

She nodded, moving from Kenton's grasp to the opposite side of the bed. Snatching a sweatshirt, she pulled it over her head, then slipped on some shoes. Kenton led her past the men and toward the steps.

The adrenaline was wearing off by the time they descended. Her body was weary and weak, and the ache in her arm intensified.

Kenton's arm went around her waist, practically holding her up as they made it to the porch.

"Come on, Olivia," he said as he swept her into his arms.

"I can walk."

"Not that well."

She leaned into him, gripping his neck and feeling much too tired to fight.

18

———

After finally getting her into the SUV, Kenton slid into the driver's seat and headed to the hospital. Hitting the button on the steering wheel, he called Marcus.

"What's happened?"

"She took out three men sent to kill her. One's still alive. If he wakes, we might be able to get something from him."

"Is she okay?"

"I'm fine. Just a scratch," she mumbled.

She leaned against the door, her face pale. Exhausted and worn out, she needed to get some rest.

"Where are you? I'm coming now."

"I'm taking her to the hospital. I think my presence helped convince the detective of the situation, but he wants to talk to you. She got nicked on the upper arm, nothing serious."

"I—"

"Marcus, stop. I'll be fine. Once I'm stitched up, I'll get a bag and head to Primrose."

"No, stay with Kenton until I come to get you. You will not spend any time alone until this clears. I've already put in a word about 'round-the-clock guards, and I think now's the time they get started."

"Marcus," she groaned.

"Sounds good. I'll call you if something else comes up." Kenton hung up before she could object further.

"I'm not staying with you."

"It's not like you're staying the night. Just until he can get free."

"How ... why did you come?"

He frowned and checked his mirrors once more, making sure they weren't followed.

"I was the one who called you. Marcus couldn't answer. He's been in a meeting with the board all evening. When I checked in with him earlier, he said he would move any calls from you to my phone until he could get free and asked me to drive by tonight. I didn't have service when you called, so when it clicked over as a missed call, I called back. I was already headed here."

Glancing over, he saw her nod, a frown on her face.

"He'll be miserable now."

"He wants to keep you safe, Olivia."

"Why?" She sighed and turned in the seat, gripping her elbow with a wince. "Why do you keep calling me that when you know my name is Ollie?"

"Your name is Olivia."

"But I don't go by that, never have."

He could feel her eyes burning into him, and he ignored it. She'd had a terrible night and was exhausted. Bringing it all up, knowing how much it annoyed her, he didn't want to do that to her tonight. If he could help it, she wouldn't return to that house at all.

"Don't you have a bag or change of clothes elsewhere we could pick up?"

She sighed. "At the office. In my car. I have an apartment in town."

"We'll go there after you get stitched up."

"You know I can do that."

"I know. I can too. But this is a police-involved case, not off the books. You need to go to the hospital."

The silence spread as they pulled into the ER and parked. After making it inside, he explained the situation and showed his badge, earning them a quicker entrance to a room.

He helped her get the sweatshirt off her arm, her hands pushing him away as he did so. She finished pulling it off and then sat down to fill out her paperwork. He found a spot against the wall, watching her in the chair since she refused to sit on the exam table. Her hair fell over her shoulders, the slim night shirt hanging loosely on her frame.

He mentally throttled himself, irritated he hadn't gotten there sooner. He never should've left in the first place. But since Marcus didn't tell him to stay, and with the tension ... he shook his head. It didn't matter. This was on him.

"This would be easier if you weren't glaring at me." She looked up.

"I'm not glaring."

"Ogling?"

He smirked as she shook her head. Huffing, she finished the papers as a doctor entered.

"Miss Lloyd, I need you up here, please."

She frowned and stood on the step before sitting on the table with a grunt.

"That's a bad cut. According to the staff, it's a police matter?"

"She was attacked. Home invasion."

The doctor snapped around with wide eyes. "Sorry, didn't see you there. Okay, well, let's get you cleaned up and out of here."

She closed her eyes as the doctor made small talk with

himself, not questioning either of them. Kenton assumed it was to make her more comfortable.

Stepping up to her right side, he took her hand, making her eyes pop open. Her jaw tensed as she focused on his chest, breathing heavily.

"Okay, there you go. Now, you can shower with due caution. They'll be fine. Just ensure you keep them aired out and avoid strenuous activities. You need to watch for infection."

"Thanks, she's got it." He nodded to the doctor, who looked between them and nodded, then left the room. "Olivia?"

"Let's go get my stuff and—"

He pushed in front of her and pulled her close as she held her left arm to her chest. She rested her head against his chest, breathing out as he rubbed her back.

"You good?"

"I'm fine. You and Marcus worry too much."

He frowned as he held her waist, squeezing. "You know, it's been a rough couple of days."

"And it'll get worse. So, let me get discharged and go get my things."

He sighed and stepped back. She slid between him and the bed, still refusing to look him in the eye. Pushing him back completely, she grabbed her sweatshirt, gripping it to her chest as he turned to follow.

She signed the discharge order, then nodded as the nurse handed her a packet, which she tossed into the trash on their way out.

Following her directions to her apartment, he wondered why she'd pushed him away so quickly. He had fully expected her to break down in the hospital room, but she hadn't. Moving in closer seemed to steel her more instead of giving her a place to rest.

"Here, you can park in my spot."

Pulling next to the curb, she got out and didn't wait as she headed down the sidewalk. Catching up, he held his tongue as they walked into the high-rise. Ignoring the turned heads, probably from her workout attire and bloody sweatshirt, they walked through the lobby and onto the elevator.

Another silent ride led them to the fifth floor, and she marched down the hall to the door. She tapped the keypad until the door lock turned green and made her way inside.

"Since I'm here, how about I stay, and you go home?" She walked to the kitchen, pulled a water bottle from the fridge and drank half of it as he followed.

He leaned against the cabinet. "No."

"I'm fine."

"Okay."

"Look, I'm secure here. Marcus knows that."

"Go grab your bag."

She narrowed her eyes, stepping in front of him. "I don't take orders."

He sighed. "I'm not ordering you. I'm asking. Besides, we both know you're not going to change my mind. The quicker we get out of here, the better."

She glared a moment before turning and marching out of the kitchen and down the hallway.

Gazing after her, he frowned. She wasn't the typical woman he dated—or even met, for that matter. After all the closeness they seemed to share, the feel of her up against him in his home, and the hug she'd so quickly offered earlier, he was struggling to let it all lie.

With the case far from over, how in the world could he remain focused and keep everything between them platonic?

Browsing the apartment, he smiled at the pictures of her and Marcus on the walls. That amazing grin of hers was captured in shot after shot, her eyes dancing and full of happiness. The pictures were mostly of her in different locations, her hair down and wild as she had most likely hiked or climbed her way to different places.

"What're you doing?"

He ignored her terse tone and ambled to another picture. "Just looking. You've been to some incredible places."

"Let's go," she muttered.

"I thought you said this was your place?"

She had already changed into jeans and a T-shirt, her back to him as she headed to the door. Her hair was once more piled on top of her head, strands falling around her face as she turned.

"I know you wouldn't have this many pictures of only you on the walls. This is someplace Marcus stays on occasion."

"What does it matter?"

He shrugged as he pushed his hands in his pockets. "Just curious. Why don't you trust me?"

"Who says I don't?"

"Look, I'm trying to ease the mood." He smiled and stepped forward, pulling the duffle from her grip.

She tensed, an action she'd suppressed in all their other interactions.

"Kenton, I ..." She let out a groan. "I don't like people hovering around me. I'm used to being alone, by myself. But as I say all that, I realize you probably understand that much more than I do."

He nodded, focusing on her alluring eyes that dodged his. "I do."

"The way Marcus ... he's going to be horrendous to deal with now. Overbearing and—"

"He's scared."

She finally looked up. Red flooded her cheeks, making her lips that much brighter as they parted. He took a calming breath.

"Olivia, the job he's done all his life, he's never feared. He didn't fear dying or fear for those around him while working. It's a life he prepared for. Fear can create problems when you're in those kinds of situations. So, having family in danger, the only family he has left, he has a fear. He'll die to protect you."

She bit her lip, her eyes searching his. "Is that why you don't have anyone around you?"

His eyebrow raised. "I imagine you already know the answer to that."

"I've done my research. Your father was absent, and your mother passed away from cancer when you were sixteen. I'm very sorry."

He nodded.

"You didn't even attend your graduation. You left after classes ended and went into the service. Your record was hard to find. A lot has been scrubbed."

He watched her for a minute, then leaned into her space, that sweet perfume flowing around them and sucking him in again as he took hold of her waist.

"What were you looking for?" he whispered.

Her arms crossed as she sighed. "I don't know. I was just looking."

She turned toward the door. Olivia doing her homework on him wasn't surprising. But at this point, he would gladly tell her anything if she would just ask.

Taking a breath, he followed her out. The feelings from the other day in his home pulsed through his body as he watched her glide to the elevator.

In his entire life, he didn't think he had ever been as attracted to someone as he was to Olivia. And the more she pushed, the more that tension built, the more he needed to find a way to make space.

Tonight would be a test.

19

———————

Heat built on Olivia's face as they pulled up to Kenton's home, the memory lingering of the last time she was here. Seeing Kenton bare-chested and feeling his warmth pushed up against her, his wet hair a mess on top of his head ...

She swallowed hard and slid from the seat, wishing the heat on her face would disappear. Kenton escorted her inside, then walked through each room and returned, tucking his gun back into its holster.

"You want to lie down?" His blue eyes searched hers.

Not trusting herself to speak, she shook her head, then walked into the living room. Seeing the large sectional that took up most of the room, she fell into the corner seat with a sigh. The plush leather was soft and worn, but her interest lay in the room. Empty walls and a large, empty bookshelf surrounded a massive rock fireplace.

The house was beautiful, and the living room comfortable, homey. Kicking off her shoes, she tucked her feet under her and leaned back.

A water bottle appeared on the coffee table.

"Thanks," she mumbled.

143

"You should rest. I don't know how long Marcus will be."

She shrugged and took a drink. "You're not much on the decorating side."

He chuckled. "I don't do decorating or personal effects. Habit."

She turned to see him leaning back in what she assumed was his usual seat at the end of the couch. He pushed his feet up on the coffee table and turned on the TV.

She rolled to her right to get a good look at him. "What do you do with all your time?"

His eyebrow rose, and he faced her. "All my time?"

"I just figured with all the non-connections you have, you had a lot of free time."

"What do you do?"

She chuckled and set the water on the coffee table, turning her focus to the TV. "I don't have free time. I'm too busy."

"Busy with what, exactly?"

"My job."

"I imagine all the hiking and climbing takes up your free time. Who do you go with?"

"Friends."

"Must be trustworthy friends."

She shook her head, trying to keep her smirk hidden. Her face heated once again as she felt him watching. The TV muted, and he stood, then sat next to her on the couch.

"Tell me, Olivia, how does one become a trustworthy friend?"

She frowned at him using her given name. With a sigh, she pushed back into the couch, trying to ease away from him. Those cobalt blues stared, a smirk on his lips.

"I lied. I go alone."

His smirk disappeared. "That's interesting."

"Why? A woman can't travel and do things on her own?"

"Of course. How does Marcus feel about all that solitary travel?"

Frowning, she yanked down her bun and pushed her hair back, ignoring the pain radiating up her arm and into her head. Wrapping the hair tie around her fingers, she chewed on her lip.

"I haven't traveled in a long time. Not since I've moved here."

"When was that?"

She looked up, trying to keep from getting wrapped up in his stare. "A little over a year ago."

He turned back to the TV, his jaw tensing. She let out a sigh. Kenton Matthews was a gorgeous man. Chiseled features and a full head of dark, wavy hair, the shadow across his jaw made her smile. Rugged and tough. She enjoyed that much more than the clean-cut he sported since he had come to work at the Institute.

"Who did you work for?"

"That's not important."

He chuckled. "Okay."

The sound returned to the TV.

She sat confused as he leaned back, propping up his legs and pushing an arm behind his head.

What was all that about? Why ask a question he knew she wouldn't answer?

Irritated, she pulled her purse into her lap, searching for the pain pills she had shoved in as she packed at the apartment. Taking a few out, she drank the rest of her water with them, then curled up.

He sat up momentarily, lifting the coffee table lid and pulling out a blanket. Draping it over her, he leaned back and propped his legs up again without a word.

"Thanks." She rested on her right side and pulled the blanket over her shoulder.

The craziness of the day wore on her as her eyelids closed. The sound of his breathing made her breathe deeper, smiling at his cologne as it filled the air. She felt at ease, and now, she finally felt tired.

As she drifted, the past pushed into her chest. It was as if she'd failed at life. God had given her Marcus when her parents passed, but as wonderful as he had been, he was gone so much. She had become so used to being alone.

Where on earth did she belong?

God, was this the plan? To fail and move from job to job only to be put in the middle of a war between Marcus and his enemy?

And if the enemy succeeded, she would be right back in limbo with no job, no plan, and no idea where to go or what to do.

Then there was Kenton.

Something rubbed against her arm, and she sat up, surprised to see Kenton sitting so close.

"Just giving you a pillow. You fell asleep," he whispered.

Mind groggy, she nodded as he pushed the pillow under her head.

"Lie down, please."

"I'm—"

"Fine. Yes, I know."

Reluctantly, she relented, lying down and feeling the blanket tucked around her as she curled up on the couch. Soothing fingers brushed her hair from her face, lulling her back to sleep.

SWALLOWING the lump in his throat, Kenton managed to pull his hand away and lean on his knees.

This was not happening. Not with her. Marcus Moore's

niece was not someone he should be thinking of like this, and the idea made him stand and pace.

Walking through the house, he double-checked the alarms and the locks, turning off all the lights and settling back on the couch beside her.

The idea of them together was crazy. Marcus knew he wasn't good enough, never would be. But the worst part was that Olivia seemed utterly oblivious. Sure, the attraction was there on both sides. He could see that flash across her eyes. But it wasn't just the fact she was a beautiful woman. She was intelligent and had a great sense about her. All of the training she'd completed, her past, it had sculpted her into a force—one that drew him closer.

Glancing down, he watched her sleep. Her red lips shining in the light of the muted television, her jaw that he wanted to caress once again down her neck ...

The ringing of his phone brought him out of his stupor. He stood and answered. "Marcus?"

"She all right?"

"Yeah. Just passed out. Her arm is stitched up, but she's exhausted."

Marcus's sigh echoed over the line. "We received another threat about an hour ago. The techs are still decrypting it."

"It doesn't match the same code as the last one?"

"Of course not. Rashid is playing with us, and I, for one, am done. I've been doing some research. I think I know where he's been hiding."

He glanced down to see Olivia still out and stepped into the hallway. "Don't do anything stupid. You can't go in alone. You know better."

"I realize that. But I'm done playing defense. He's about to feel some offense from me, and it's coming in the morning. I've got my own worker bees that will do what's necessary."

Kenton ground his teeth, trying to ease his temper and his

tone. Marcus had a reputation for going off. Crossing him was a very, very bad idea.

"Marcus, think about the consequences first. Just think everything through. I'm mad, too, but we have to go easy here. We're in-country, not on the outskirts of some rebel nation."

"I understand that. But these attacks, I can't handle them," Marcus hissed through the line.

He sighed. "Keep me updated. She's good for now. If you want me to move her, let me know."

"No. Let her sleep. If I don't contact you by morning, assume I've had my own work to take care of and make sure she gets to the office safely. I appreciate all you've done, more than you know."

"I told you that you don't have to thank me."

Marcus chuckled. "She hasn't been too terrible, has she?"

He smiled and glanced toward the living room, the view of her legs sticking out of the blanket visible. "No, not at all."

"I told you, run for your money."

"And I told you—"

"Yes. Yes, you did."

The silence lingered.

"Take care of her, Kenton."

"I will."

The call ended. Shoving the phone into his pocket, he sat next to Olivia, scrubbing his hand down his face.

"Where's Marcus?" Her sleepy voice made him turn.

Her eyes barely open, she looked up, a smile playing on her lips.

Man, oh man, he was in trouble.

He cleared his throat. "He's still at the office. There was another email they're trying to decode."

No sense in worrying her about his other dealings, not until he knew for sure Marcus had carried them out.

She sighed, shifting on the couch and sitting up on her

elbow. Her light brown hair hung over her shoulder as she finally focused on him.

"He's safe?"

"Probably safer there than anywhere else."

"I was hoping he'd come here. Stay with us."

He smiled at the word. Us. That was new, and he liked the thought way too much. "If he doesn't show, I'll take you to work in the morning. You sure you want to stay out here instead of the spare bedroom?"

"Are you staying out here?"

He nodded. There was no way he would be sleeping tonight.

"Then I'll stay." She laid back down, her arm stretching out with a grimace.

He pulled the blanket up. Gripping her outstretched hand, he settled into the couch and propped his feet up. Rubbing his thumb across her fingers, he heard her breathing deepen and slow in no time.

"What am I doing?" he muttered under his breath as he felt that stir again.

Leaning down, he pushed the hair from her face, lightly tracing her ear before sitting up. She trusted him to be with her, even while she was vulnerable. There was no way he would mess that up. But man, keeping his hands to himself was getting harder and harder.

"God, please help me out here. I need strength to keep focused. Please watch over Marcus. Ease his anger so he does the right thing." He glanced at Olivia again. "Protect Olivia, guard her, send Your angels to watch over her. Provide for her where I fail."

Rubbing his forehead, he sat back, still gripping her hand but feeling more in control as he blew out a ragged breath. This was going to be a long night.

20

—————

Saturday Morning

Olivia sat up with a start, looking over the empty shelves and living room. The feel of the leather under her fingertips reminded her she was at Kenton's house.

With a sigh, she fell back into the cushion, covering her face with the blanket. Man, she hadn't slept that well since the threat on the Institute. A smile stretched across her face. To be here in his house was oddly comforting.

"You finally awake?"

The smell of coffee permeated the blanket, and she grinned wider.

"Yes."

His deep chuckle warmed her heart. "Come on, sit up. I brought coffee."

"You're one of those morning people, aren't you?"

He chuckled again. "Part of the job."

She batted at the hand tugging the blanket. "Kenton, stop. I'm a mess," she said as he pulled her hand to sit up.

As the blanket fell, she did her best to smooth her hair. A

coffee mug appeared before her, and she took it with both hands.

"Thanks," she mumbled and took a sip.

"Sleep well?"

She nodded, her eyes drifting up to his. Sitting on the coffee table, he leaned in and held another mug between his hands as he intently watched her. His blue eyes searched her face, a grin forming on his lips.

"What?"

He shook his head and took a sip. "Nothing, Olivia. Not a thing."

She groaned and stood, setting the mug down next to him as she hurried past to the hallway. Grabbing her duffle from the bench he'd set it on last night, she made her way to the bathroom and slammed the door shut.

Dropping the bag on the floor, she gripped the sink and breathed out. This wasn't happening. Her whole life, she had never had this kind of ease with a man. The attraction, the delightful tension ...

After already making plans to leave, she was suddenly in over her head with a fascinating and attentive man.

She glanced in the mirror and let out a groan. Her hair was a mess, and the bruises were now obvious as the makeup she'd applied last night had scrubbed off, probably on Kenton's couch.

"Olivia?"

She jumped at Kenton's voice.

"If you want to shower, there are towels in the cabinet."

"Thanks."

She waited until his footsteps faded, then grabbed a washcloth from the cabinet to scrub her face. A shower could wait until she got to the office, but she needed to wake up.

After changing clothes, she pulled her hair into a high ponytail and applied the much-needed makeup. Taking a deep breath, she rushed through the bathroom door and dropped the bag back on the bench.

"Hungry?"

She nodded and pushed past him to the kitchen. Sitting down at a small pub table, she selected a bagel from the fare he had stacked on the table. Her coffee mug appeared in front of her.

"Thanks. You didn't have to go to the trouble. We could've just stopped somewhere." She finally looked up as he sat beside her, a curl on his lips.

"Had it all here. No trouble."

She smiled and took a bite. "Did you sleep at all?"

He shrugged and took a sip, then set the mug back on the table, focusing on the cup. "I got enough to get me through."

She chuckled. "That's not much, I imagine."

"Done more with less."

"I thought you were too old for those days."

His eyebrow rose as he smirked, making her laugh.

"Sorry, couldn't help it." She wiped her mouth and propped her elbows on the table, holding the mug to her face. "It's your joke, you know."

"Yeah, I guess it is." His gaze moved across the kitchen, and she wondered if he really felt as if he were too old to do anything with his life. Even if he felt as if his body had aged, from the video of him when he rescued her, she didn't see anything old about him. Then there was yesterday ...

She sighed. Now was not the time.

"You good?"

With a nod, she swallowed her bite. "I'm wondering why we are safe here. If Rashid is that competent and knows you're helping, don't you think he knows exactly where to look?"

"I'm not in a private, gated estate excluded from the community. Although I don't doubt he would send someone to try something, there are a lot of cameras in this neighborhood, a lot of collateral damage that would gain attention. He doesn't want that kind of attention because it would come with a federal stamp of approval."

"He knows if federal steps in, he'll have to go into hiding?"

He nodded, his gaze focused on her. Completely.

"What about taking me in the middle of the highway?"

"It was probably the only way to get to you. You're heavily armed and not someone they can simply snatch from the parking garage."

The garage.

"What?" His eyes narrowed. "You just remembered something."

"How on earth … ?"

He chuckled. "I know you better than you think, Olivia."

Resisting the urge to smile at his grin, she sipped her coffee. "When I was leaving Thursday afternoon, I thought someone was watching me in the garage. I need to look over the security tapes from that afternoon."

He set down his mug. "That's concerning."

Her gaze darted away from his as she stood and put her empty plate in the sink. She finished her coffee and set the mug in as well, turning to run into him.

"Sorry," she muttered.

He shifted, keeping her from leaving his space. "How's the arm?"

"It's fine. Just a little sore." She managed a smile before sidestepping him again.

Releasing a breath that he let her go, she gathered her duffle and purse from the hallway.

"I've already checked the car. Let's go." He took the duffle off her shoulder and led her outside and to the SUV, opening and closing the door for her before pushing her bag into the back.

Lord, please let me get through all of this without mucking things up. I don't know why You brought Kenton into my life right now, but please, please give me something else to think about.

She sighed as he slid into his seat. Too many things planned would fall apart if she couldn't get her head together. The Institute and the hack, her possible position in the UK, and then, of course, Kenton Matthews.

Biting her lip, she swallowed hard and tried to steel herself. Losing her heart to Kenton wasn't part of the plan. She couldn't stand to lose one more person, lose one more part of her heart to anyone.

This was going to be a long weekend.

21

———

Kenton grinned as they drove in silence.

Olivia was rattled, and for some reason, he enjoyed the sight. The always cool and calm Olivia Lloyd was captivating to watch as she handled people and situations. But it made his heart pound to see her like this with him.

After thinking about their tension-filled situation last night, he decided there was little he could change. Until Rashid was caught and the threat gone, he planned on sticking as close to her as possible. Even if that meant teeing up for a little more of the game she seemed to enjoy playing with him.

"What's that grin for?"

He shrugged. "Just hopeful we'll get what we need today."

"Hmff." She scoffed. "That would be a miracle."

"Did Marcus ever tell you what happened after we first met?" He glanced over and smiled as she leaned into the console between them.

"No. What happened?"

He checked his mirrors and shifted lanes. "The fact we got out was a miracle. We were sitting there, getting ready to die, and he said he should pray." His gaze cut to that smile on her lips. "I said there was no point. He said if we made it out, we would have to have a conversation." He paused and took a breath, remembering the state of his life back then.

"I told him I might just consider it if we did make it out, because it would be a miracle." He chuckled. "Once we made it, he used the entire hour drive to tell me about Christ and how He saved us just so I wouldn't die without Him."

Her hand gripped his forearm, and he stilled.

"Marcus never mentioned that." Her voice was soft as his arm tingled under her touch.

"It's true. If it weren't for Marcus, I think we would've died, and that would've been that." He swallowed as her thumb rubbed across his skin.

"So, what kind of life did you have before?"

He shrugged. "The kind where I did what I wanted and didn't care about much. It wasn't like I had a family or connections to deal with or anyone to lecture me. I felt no guilt, and honestly, I'm surprised God even cared one way or the other that I got saved." He chuckled. "I was more than lost. I was alone. It made everything I did easier."

"And now?"

That toying voice of hers made him smile.

"And now, I'm completely different. Ten years later, and I'm still shocked that I have someone who cares anything about me or what I do."

"Kenton, surely you have friends who care what you do."

He shrugged. "I do have friends. But those guys are few and far between. Besides, I never really see them."

The silence spread for a while, and her thumb stopped moving across his arm.

"I didn't mean it earlier. You're not too old," she murmured.

"I know." He chuckled.

"Then ..." Her hand slid from his arm. "Then why aren't you married and living it up here in the States?"

He grinned and glanced at the laughter on her face. "It's not that I haven't tried. But as you know, my past creates problems."

"You really think you have enemies ready to come for you after this long?"

"Never know. But my past is hard to explain. When I get close to a woman, she asks about my previous job, what I used to do. What do I say then? There's a roadmap on my body. It's not an easy conversation."

Her green eyes found his for a second before he turned back to the road.

"And you've actually experienced that conversation?"

He grimaced.

"I think there's something else there. Like you've decided you don't deserve anyone, a future, so you hide away."

"You think I'm hiding?"

She shrugged. "I just wonder how often you date and then drop that same woman because you know she wasn't right in the first place. It gives you a wonderful excuse to hide and look like you're trying."

Heat flooded his face, and he shook his head. "What makes you think I do that?"

"Just an observation."

Bruno's dead.

After parking, he escorted her inside, keeping her close and working to keep his focus on the area and not her body pushed against his. Entering the lobby, she pulled away.

"I need to go take care of things in my office. I'm sure you have things to do." She pushed the elevator button as she glanced over her shoulder at him.

"As a matter of fact, I do."

The elevator ride was silent as usual, but as she stepped onto the second floor, he took her hand. "You won't leave the building, right?"

She frowned.

"Olivia. Promise you won't leave without me. Call me first."

Her green eyes searched his face, finally nodding. "I promise."

He squeezed her fingers, reluctantly letting her go as she pulled away. Pausing in the hallway, he took a breath. Now was not the time. He had a job to do and a partner to kill.

Slamming the door into the wall, he glared down at Bruno sitting at the table.

"What's wrong now?"

"What kind of talk did you and Olivia have?"

Bruno frowned. "What does that mean?"

"Don't." He stepped in front of his partner, hands clenched and working to keep from pounding the guy.

Bruno was one of the only men he worked with whom he considered a close friend. But now, he was finding too many reasons to cut ties.

"Look, she asked about you, had questions. I just tried to ease her off."

"Ease her off?" Kenton gritted his teeth.

"She asked. I answered."

"Asked what, exactly?"

"How long we've been working together. Why I thought you weren't looking to settle down."

"You said that?"

Bruno shrugged. "I said you dated but hadn't had much luck."

Kenton paced, raking his hand through his hair. "Brune, wasn't your place to say a word. Not one word."

"I know, and I'm sorry. But she's ... there's something about her. She has a lot of stuff hidden."

He scoffed. "Her uncle is a former SAS member, and she probably followed his career or training at some point. You better watch your back, man. She'll eat you up."

Bruno nodded. "Yeah, sorry. Really, I wasn't thinking." A

smile crossed his face. "But that just means you have something for her, don't you?"

"Not the time. We have a case, and she's a target. I'm much more concerned with keeping her safe and stopping the hack."

"I got it, but what now? Coleston isn't talking, and I can't find anything that would give us probable cause to go through his computer. If he's the mole and used Downing, we can't prove it."

"How's the program you and Olivia started yesterday?"

Bruno shrugged. "I've been sifting through the people that the program highlighted, but if we expect Coleston and he was online, we need a way to get into his system first. He's had us blocked out since we first ran the program."

Kenton sat down. "I'll ask Marcus about that when I see him. He spoke with the board last night, so maybe it'll get us somewhere. How's the system look?"

"So far, it's perfect. I don't have any reason to think someone from the outside could get in."

Leaning back, he crossed his arms. "I hate to say it, but I don't have anything else to do unless we get a specific—"

"Kenton."

Olivia strode through the door, wearing a change of clothes and a glare.

"Olivia."

"Why didn't you tell me?"

He frowned. "Tell you what?"

"Marcus is gone. He's out hunting Rashid on his own."

He jumped up and took her elbow, leading her out of the room. "Keep running it, Bruno," he called over his shoulder as he led her to the elevator. "How do you know?"

She ripped her arm from his grip. "I found a message on my office phone."

When the elevator opened, he led her inside and hit the button for Marcus's floor.

"I didn't know he was going alone. He said he had others looking into it."

Her face went red. "You know him well enough to know he'd go off and find him."

He pushed into her space. "He told me he wouldn't. Marcus has a temper, but he's also intelligent. He wouldn't go in alone." His jaw set as she turned away, shaking her head and gripping her arms, her damp hair hanging over her shoulders. "Olivia."

"Don't." Her stern voice hit his heart, a lump forming in his throat.

As the doors opened, they darted to Marcus's office, and she punched in the code to get inside. The room was empty as she rushed to Marcus's computer and sat down, opening it up.

"You know his codes?"

"He's got a few places pulled up ..." Her finger rubbed across her bottom lip.

He pulled out his phone and called Marcus's cell.

"Kenton."

"Where are you?"

A deep sigh sounded as Olivia jumped up and reached for the phone. Kenton pushed her hand away.

"I've been working on details. Finding a trail."

"Olivia is upset."

Marcus's sigh sounded again. "I'm sorry. I was hoping to be back by now."

He pulled the phone down, gripping her hand as she reached again. "He's fine. He's not after Rashid."

She tried to pull away, but he pressed her hand against his chest, lifting the phone once more.

"So, you're on your way back, right?"

Shifting his hand to her waist, he pulled her in, her eyes darting back and forth between his.

"Yes, I should be there soon. Is everything all right? Did you have any problems?"

"Everything is fine. No problems. Find Olivia as soon as you get here."

"I will. Thank you."

"Not an issue."

Kenton hung up, tension gripping his shoulders. He was waiting for her to push him off, back away, do something to end the stalemate they found themselves in. Because right now, he didn't think he could step away.

"Kenton."

As he pocketed his phone, he took her elbow, rubbing his thumb against her smooth skin as his other hand ran across her back, pulling her in even more.

"Are you done?" she whispered, her lips parted as she kept her focus.

"Not even close." He grinned as she sighed.

"With the case."

As much as he didn't want to admit it, they seemed to have hit a dead end. Without a lead that could give them something to work toward, there was nothing else he could do as a detective.

"Let's see what Bruno comes up with."

She nodded as they stood together, neither shifting to leave. He brushed some strands of hair from her face, pushing them behind her ear and trailing his finger to her jaw. With great effort, he let his hand fall, pocketing it with a sigh.

"I need to get back to work."

He nodded. "Marcus will come find you as soon as he arrives."

She searched his face again, opening her mouth as if she wanted to speak, but nothing came out. Her brows furrowed, and she spun around. Watching her leave, he swallowed as pain hit his gut. Not making a move seemed to upset her, but now wasn't the time.

As easy as he found everyone to read, she remained a

mystery. She liked to play games, used silence to create tension, and let others assume what they wanted. But there was so much more under the surface, the little bit of emotion he got to see this morning and last night. He wanted more.

Hands in his pockets, he walked out of the room and leaned against the wall to wait for the elevator. Besides, if she was leaving after all of this, then what was the point in pushing for anything more? He'd just have to enjoy the game she played, hopefully finding a way to reel himself in when she did decide to leave.

Stepping into the elevator, he hit the button and sighed. If Rashid was still after the data on the servers, and Bruno was certain they were secure from the outside, would he risk using the same mole to upload the information?

The cat-and-mouse of it all was something Kenton excelled at. If he knew there was a target and someone was going to make a move, he usually could cinch it up. But with Rashid and the technological heist he was planning, Kenton's knowledge was limited.

Pushing into the workroom, he found Bruno still at the table.

"I want everything you have on Coleston. All the video, audio if you have it, everything from that day and the few days previous. We need to track his movements, see if he did something out of character."

"Got it."

Feeling helpless, Kenton paced the room. The attack was set to happen tomorrow at midnight, and they were no closer than when they started. It was the same with every case Rashid was a part of. There would be no evidence. Only silenced loose ends and missing intel. The thought angered him.

"You good?"

He sighed. "Just thinking."

"About what?"

"If Rashid gets what he needs, what happens to Marcus and Olivia?"

Bruno slowly shook his head. "Don't know."

"We need to nail him, Brune. We need something to either force the mole to cooperate or find a link to Rashid."

"I know. We'll find something. Don't worry."

With Marcus on the warpath, if they didn't get a line on Rashid, the real concern was Marcus doing something Kenton couldn't help counter.

"Is Rashid still wanted by Homeland or the FBI?"

"Let me see." Bruno clicked away. "He's not on a watch list, and his name isn't flagging. It could just be because they don't anticipate him being in the US. Since I don't have an actual report of him being in the States, and all we have is yours and Marcus's affirmation that he's the hacker, it's not like I can call in a sighting and ask if the feds want to step in."

"Yeah, I figured." His phone buzzed, and he pulled it from his pocket. "Yeah?"

"Marcus is back and wants to speak to us in his office."

"I'm on my way." He frowned as Olivia hung up on him.

"Problem?"

Kenton shook his head. "I'm going to speak to Marcus." He headed toward the door.

22

———

Pacing the room, Olivia watched as Marcus sat frowning at his computer. He swore up and down that he had been careful and hadn't engaged anyone. But he had gone out alone, to find Rashid, and that terrified her.

As much as she trusted her uncle, it was hard to believe he hadn't been found out or close to Rashid. The fact Rashid had gone after her twice now was something Marcus would take personally, and it was only a matter of time before Marcus did something about it.

"So, what's the news?"

She paused to watch Kenton stalk in, glaring at Marcus. His blue eyes shifted to hers for only a moment. She shouldn't be upset with him, but the fact he refused to tell her that Marcus had been after revenge was more than frustrating.

Plus, the fact he didn't even make the slightest attempt to kiss her earlier made her feel slighted. Not that right then was the best time to kiss, in Marcus's office, in the middle of all this mess ...

"Olivia has some ideas, but I wanted to speak to both of you about my meetings with the board last night."

She leaned against the desk, facing Marcus and putting her back to Kenton. "And what did they have to say?"

Marcus stroked his chin before linking his fingers on his lap. "They won't pressure Coleston without more proof. Your word and suspicions aren't enough, I'm afraid. Unless we can get something concrete, they will not allow us to search his computer without his authorization."

"What about the gear he used to block us? That's not protocol." She stood and pushed her hands on her hips.

"Yes, I discussed that at length, tried to use it to our advantage. Clearly, the man has something to hide. They decided on a two-week suspension without pay. He was called and questioned about the devices. He simply stated he had important documents and blueprints he didn't want anyone to have access to. The fact his device affected our audio and video signals was unknown to him."

She scoffed. "What a liar." She gritted her teeth and paced.

"Martin, on the other hand, is being investigated."

"What for?" Kenton's deep voice echoed in the large office.

"The email he received about Downing proved to be a fraud. Downing was, in fact, fired from his previous position, and when I called and spoke with his superior, the man was quite adamant that we look at everything he had his hands in.

"Downing stole a few things from his previous employer, and by the time they discovered it, he was on to bigger and pricier items. Projects had to be scrapped, started over because he messed with the coding. He basically held the technology hostage until he was paid. They simply paid him off and fired him. He left, and they didn't press charges."

Her mouth dropped. "Why wouldn't they press charges? That's ludicrous."

"Bad PR."

She looked over at Kenton.

His gaze held hers. "If the press got wind, their company

could be defunded. Backers would bail, worried their money would be compromised."

"So, why did Martin hire him?"

"He says he received the email from a friend who worked with Downing, gave him a great reference even though he was listed as fired. His friend stated it was all a misunderstanding. But Drone took a look at the email, backtraced it, and discovered it was phony. It originated from Martin's home computer."

"So, why would Martin risk it?" Kenton made his way to the edge of Marcus's desk, leaning a hip against it with crossed arms.

"Money. Drone's not certain, but he thinks Martin was given a large sum of money to get Downing hired on."

"You know, I remember hearing about him buying a boat or something like that." As Olivia paced, she held her chin, pushing at her bottom lip. "I didn't think much of it at the time, but the man seems much too ordinary for a sailboat."

Kenton scoffed.

She paused with a frown. "What?"

"You have to have a certain way about you to own a boat?"

"Actually, yes. There are people who sail, and there are people who do not. Martin most definitely does not. But a pricy boat could be what he needed to find someone who might be interested."

"You?" Kenton grinned, and she shook her head.

"Not a chance," she muttered and started her pacing again. "So much for my interviewing him before he gets suspended."

Kenton took his time looking from her to Marcus. "So, Downing manipulated the system to get hired. How did Coleston connect with him?"

Marcus shrugged. "Not sure, but the fact they hit it off seems curious."

Her hands dropped to her sides. "None of this matters. If we can't connect Coleston to Rashid, then we have nothing to go with, nothing to legally stop Rashid or Coleston from doing whatever they're planning."

"We might have something."

She turned to see Bruno and Drone rush in with broad smiles.

"I hope it's good news," Kenton said.

"We might have found enough probable cause to convince the board to let us dig a little deeper into Coleston."

Bruno set down the laptop, and she walked around, pushing in front of Kenton to see it. His hand pulled her forward, gripping her waist.

"Kenton wanted all the video of Coleston processed, and we found this."

Coleston sat at Downing's desk, working on the system. The time stamp put the occurrence well before anyone other than security would arrive.

"This is the day after the breach. He's not usually on the floor, so a security guard spoke with him. The guard said he claimed to need to do a reset on his system and all the computers in his unit."

She frowned. "That doesn't prove much. It's odd, but not enough."

Bruno nodded. "Remember that program we created?"

"Yes. Kenton said you saw Coleston online at the time of the breach."

"We did. So, this is the day after the breach. He was using the flash drive. The video shows him pulling something from the side and palming it. It could be he took something off Downing's computer, put it on the flash drive, and used it later."

"We need to talk to Downing."

She turned to see the stern expression on Kenton's face. "You think he'll talk?"

He shrugged. "If I'm right, we might just get enough

information to prove to the board that Coleston is up to something."

Pulling her mouth to the side, she nodded. "So, you think Downing is the mole, but Coleston beat him to it for some reason?"

Kenton nodded. "What if all the discussions Downing and Coleston had, those we saw on the video and others, were because Coleston suspected something?"

"That makes sense."

She looked at Bruno.

"Monte, go get Downing and set him up in one of the rooms. Detective Price, you have full access to Downing's computer. Do you know what to look for?"

"Yes, sir. I'll get started."

Monte and Bruno left the room, but what would Bruno be looking for? Kenton's hand moved across the small of her back as she turned.

As if he knew, Kenton caught her focus. "If Coleston found out that Downing had intentions to sabotage the company or found a way to allow Rashid access, he might've searched his computer. He might even decide he should be the one to gain from the hack while setting up Downing to take the fall."

"It's a perfect plan." She glanced from Kenton to Marcus.

"Let's see what Bruno can find on Downing's computer, then we'll have more to go after Downing with."

"I'll get eyes on Coleston. We need to make sure he doesn't contact Rashid. You can call me when Bruno is done, and we're ready to interrogate Downing." Kenton looked to her. "Which means you'll stay in the office, right?"

Her jaw flexed as she glared. "I don't need to be put in my place, detective."

His cheeks turned red. "Olivia."

Darting past the desk and ignoring Kenton, she slammed the door against the wall and headed to the stairs.

Pushing through the door, she rushed downstairs, her face burning and her anger rising. It was bad enough he felt the need to act like that when it was just the two of them, but there was no reason to voice such a demand in front of Marcus.

Rushing to her door, the ding and swish of the elevator opening made her shake her head.

"Olivia."

She ignored Kenton's call as she pushed into her office and slammed the door closed, listening to the automatic lock engage.

"Olivia, open the door."

"I'm too busy. You'll have to excuse me. You know I have to take every precaution to stay safe."

She gritted her teeth and hoped her tone was enough to make him leave. Sitting at her desk, she pulled up the blacked-out copies of Halil Rashid's file from Marcus's computer. She wasn't surprised he had access to such materials, but how easily she found them was concerning.

The door opened, and Kenton marched toward her desk, a stern glare on his face. She minimized the screen.

"How did you get the code?"

"Didn't need it."

She stood and glared. "Kenton, how did you get into my office?"

He shrugged. "You really weren't going to let me in, were you?" His eyes narrowed as she crossed her arms.

"Why should I?"

He sighed and walked around her desk, pushing her chair out of the way to take hold of her arms. Her body stiffened, unwilling to allow the attraction between them to dampen her anger.

"I'm sorry."

She continued to glare into his deep blue eyes. Why did he have to look so amazing?

"Olivia, I'm truly sorry. It came out before I could stop it. You know this thing between us is just going to keep growing. And as long as Rashid is out there, I'm going to be concerned."

Working to keep from biting her cheek at his revelation, she dropped her gaze to his chest.

"Okay, maybe it's too much of a jump for you to admit, but there is definitely something between us," he whispered.

She cleared her throat. "No excuses. I'm tired of being patronized. I understand what you and Marcus have seen is terrifying, and I'm trying to be flexible here, but being told what to do like a child—"

"I'm apologizing. I understand why you're upset. But just know, I'm upset about all this too. I don't want you to be a target, and until Rashid is caught, I'm afraid that's exactly what you are. Marcus sees it too ..." he trailed off as she gripped the front of his sport coat, keeping her focus away from his eyes.

"Fine, go do your job, and let me do mine." Releasing his coat, she tried to step back, but his hands held her tight. "Kenton."

He sighed and pulled her in, wrapping her up in a hug. As mad as she wanted to be, she couldn't resist wrapping her arms around him.

He chuckled. "Wasn't sure you'd forgive me, Olivia."

"It's Ollie," she muttered as he laughed.

Planting a quick kiss on her head, he released her and hurried away, not even looking back as he left her office.

She collapsed in her chair with a sigh. As much as she didn't want to be pleased he'd come to apologize, it was too much of an effort to ignore. Biting the inside of her cheek, she smiled as his words filled her mind and her heart. If he was feeling as much between them ...

"Get focused. You have a job to do and then a move to make after this is all over." She pulled herself up to the desk to go over the security videos from Friday.

Heart still pounding, she ran the program, watching each car driving into and out of the garage.

Wishing for something else wasn't even an option. She already had plans, and they didn't include Kenton Matthews. No matter how much heat moved between them, how attractive he was, and how much she loved having his strong arms wrapping her up.

Her thoughts were interrupted. A grainy figure appeared on the screen and moved from the street into the garage. The figure crouched behind a car, disappearing into the shadows. Fast forwarding to when she left, a slight movement caught her attention. The video proved she'd looked directly at the shadow and hadn't seen anyone.

Knowing Rashid was targeting her to get into the system was one thing. She could easily understand that tactic. But Kenton and Marcus had been pushing for her protection to the point it never made sense. Now it did.

Rashid was not just targeting the system. He was going after her.

Changing the dates to today, she watched as she and Kenton entered the building. Snatching up the phone, she pressed the code to contact security. They needed to tighten up if someone was trying ....

As the video played on, another figure slid into the garage. The phone continued to ring.

Why was security not answering the phone?

23

With a grin, Kenton pushed through the elevator to the parking deck, pulling his keys from his pocket. Olivia was on his mind, and it had taken a lot of restraint to only kiss her on the head. But if he wanted to catch Rashid, his focus had to improve, or he would be in loads of trouble.

As he grabbed the SUV's door handle, he paused. Taking a deep breath, he dropped the handle and pulled out his phone, calling Marcus.

"Kenton?"

"Yeah, I just thought of something." He pocketed his hand and moved away from the SUV. "I think we might be looking at this wrong."

"What? Where are you?"

Kenton ignored the question and spoke urgently. "No, I don't think so. We need to focus on the hack."

"Be there in a minute."

The phone clicked in his ear as he hit the button on the elevator. Turning slightly, he pulled his weapon from his back and dropped his phone to aim at the SUV. Hitting the driver's side back window, he shot four times, then paused.

A sudden barrage of bullets let loose, and he ducked behind another vehicle.

Straining, he sat up and fired his weapon several more times, ignoring the pain shooting into his side.

"Kenton!"

Olivia's voice took his focus. She kneeled behind a car, gun aimed. With a nod, he fired as he sprinted across the garage, straight to Olivia, who gave him cover.

"What're you doing here?" He collapsed beside her and released the empty clip, pushing a new one in.

"I was studying the security cameras and saw someone enter," she grumbled as she returned fire. "The security guard never answered the phone. How many?"

"Just one, I think."

He rose and fired at the back window, turning to see Marcus come off the elevator with a rifle aimed and blasting. He chuckled and stood, moving in behind Marcus.

The shooting ended, and he opened the back door. One man sat slumped over, falling out of the door as another was half in half out of the back.

"You carry that with you here, too, huh?" He grinned at Marcus, who finally found a slight smile.

"You know it's my favorite gun."

"What on earth are you two talking about?" Olivia stood behind them, her pant leg torn and her hand on her hip.

He shook his head. "Call the cops?"

"On their way."

Olivia approached the SUV. "How did you know they were there?" Her bright green eyes centered on his.

"Cologne. Someone was wearing a strong cologne." He frowned, eyeing her torn pant leg. "You weren't supposed to leave the building."

She glared. "I looked over the cameras from the other day and noticed someone enter. When I switched to today, another figure showed. When I couldn't get the security guard to answer, I headed down."

He bit his tongue, wanting to tell her exactly how bad it would've been if she had been the one to come out first, but the worry on her face proved she already knew.

Wrapping an arm around her waist, he guided her to the elevators. "Come on. I'll take you back upstairs."

"The police should be here soon. I'll have them wait in the lobby for you."

He nodded at Marcus, whose grim frown suggested the timetable for offense just got pushed up. Escorting her into the elevator, she sighed and holstered her weapon as he did. Crossing her arms, she bit her lip, her jaw moving back and forth, and something more than worry covering her features.

In silence, he led her to her office, where she put in her code and pushed through the door.

"Look, I had no idea you were even down there, and I ..."

He shut the door and pulled her into his arms. It didn't take long for her to grip his sides, her body shaking.

Rubbing her back, he squeezed her tight, breath stolen by the feeling of her pushing into him and holding him in return. It had been far too long since he felt something more than a pleasant attraction, and it rocked him to his core. He was falling hard for this woman.

She tried to push away, but he held her tighter. Wiping her face, she groaned.

"I'm fine, Kenton. You have things to do."

"This is more important."

"Yes, I'm sure my blubbering is more important than catching Coleston making contact with Rashid."

He sighed and pulled her hands from her face, pushing her palms against his chest. "This is much more important. Tell me what's going on."

Brushing some hair from her face, he grinned when she kept her hand on his chest, gripping his coat.

"I was just surprised and then I noticed the holes in your SUV. I called for you, but you didn't answer." She looked up and furrowed her brows. "Why're you smiling?"

"Just enjoying the fact you're here, trusting me. I guess I didn't hear you call at first. As soon as I did, I came to find you."

She frowned. "You should've stayed where you were. You could've ..." Her eyes went wide as they dropped from his. "You've been shot."

He glanced down as she pulled open his coat. A bloody streak appeared on his side, across his ribcage.

"It's just a scratch, I'm sure."

"Kenton," she groaned. "Do you have to make everything so difficult? You need a paramedic."

"No. It's in a spot I can get to. I'll take care of it."

He pulled her hand from his side, shaking his head with a smile.

"What now?"

He let out a heavy sigh, holding both of her hands in his. "Nothing, Olivia. It's nothing."

After years of being alone, tending to his own wounds and living for himself, having her worrying over him and wanting to help was almost too much to handle.

"You are the most frustrating man." She yanked free and crossed her arms, standing there glaring at him, and all he could do was smile.

"Don't be mad. With everything going on, I don't want you to be upset." His gaze caught the red seeping from her arm. With a frown, he pulled up the sleeve on her left arm. "You've busted a stitch."

"Oh, and that's more important than the fact you were shot?"

"I know this was unexpected, and I'm sorry I didn't answer

you. I didn't mean to scare you." He pushed back into her space, holding her injured arm steady.

"You didn't scare me," she muttered. "You need to see someone."

He sighed, pulling her gently with him. "We both do. Come on."

His hand moved to her waist again as if some force called to him, pulling him toward her. And the way things were going, he wasn't positive he was wrong.

24

———————

At the hospital, Olivia sat in the hallway and waited for Kenton to come out of the exam room. Her stitch had been an easy fix, but Kenton's injury was much worse. The police had already been around to get her statement as well as Kenton's, which left her wondering.

Sitting in the waiting area, she leaned back and crossed her arms, feeling off. This whole thing seemed like it was toying with them. If Rashid wanted her, or Marcus for that matter, he could've mounted an attack by now, and they would've been unprepared. But sending only two men after a highly trained man like Kenton was odd.

Would Rashid normally mess around? Play games, just to get Marcus and Kenton off balance?

Rubbing her finger across her bottom lip, she stared into space and tried to figure out their point of attack. They needed answers sooner rather than later. Even if they got Downing to talk about Coleston, that didn't mean it would track back to Rashid. And he was the one they needed to stop.

"That's your thinking face. What's on your mind?"

Looking up, Kenton had a smile on his face.

"I'm thinking about the case. How're you?"

He collapsed into the chair next to her. "Better now that I know someone is sitting here with you. You shouldn't be out here alone. I wasn't happy when you walked off after we arrived."

She sighed and tried to hold back her irritation. After every attack and strain, she needed to see things from his better-trained perspective.

"Nothing to say?"

She shook her head as his hand enveloped hers, interlacing their fingers.

"Then let's get out of here." He helped her stand, and they walked hand in hand to the elevators before she let go.

Leaning against the back wall, she tried to ease the emotions welling up inside. He had been through so much, yet he took it all in stride as if the recent attacks were nothing more than commonplace annoyances.

His arm went around her as they exited the elevator and walked outside. Marcus had sent a driver to pick them up, and after Kenton asked a few questions, they climbed inside.

He sighed and leaned his head back, closing his eyes.

"Are you asleep?" she whispered.

"Almost," he muttered back.

Pulling at his arm, she wrapped hers around it and leaned into him. His breathing eased. The last night of no sleep had obviously done him in. With all the excitement, it was a wonder he was functioning.

Tracing his fingers, she felt the bumps and scars across his skin and on his bones. His hands had protected her, but they seemed much gentler now.

With a sigh, she closed her eyes and prayed.

Lord, please protect Kenton. He'll die to protect me and Marcus. Don't let him leave this world because of us. Thank You for sending him to us, giving us a chance to get to know one another, and please guide us to the end of this tunnel.

WAKING, Kenton started to sit up when he realized Olivia was sleeping against his shoulder, her arms wrapped around his. He squeezed her hand, leaning down and kissing her head. As he breathed her in, he smiled.

She had already kicked off her shoes, legs pulled up next to her and face turned up. Those red lips tempted him, and he sighed. She was much too beautiful to be with a guy like him. But as much as he had tried, it seemed God had a different plan.

The car stopped, and he saw the Institute's front entrance out his window.

"Pull around to the garage. The executive entrance."

"Yes, sir."

The car started up and moved again.

Looking down, he brushed the hair from her face, making her wake. Those green eyes opened, focusing on him.

"Oh, I didn't mean to fall asleep." She sat up, pulling away.

"Hey." He grabbed her hand, and she stilled. "You okay?"

She put on a fake smile and nodded, then let go of his hand to slide her shoes back on.

"Here you go."

He looked around and pushed out the door, watching the area as Olivia slid from the seat. Slamming the car door, he moved her to the waiting elevator and led her inside.

"How's your side?"

"It's fine. I'm more worried about you."

Instead of becoming irritated, she only nodded and turned to face the door. As the elevator opened, he escorted her to her office, letting her input the code and open the door.

She sighed heavily, walking inside and sitting against the edge of her desk as he shut the door.

"So, now what?"

He frowned. "I'm going to check on Bruno, then get eyes on Coleston."

Stepping in front of her, he pocketed his hands, doing his best to keep from pulling her up into his arms. His focus was squarely on Olivia, and with Rashid working harder than he expected to get to them, that had to change.

"I'm worried about Marcus." Olivia crossed her arms, her glassy eyes staring up at him. "He's already gone out on his own to look for Rashid. After all this, I'm afraid of what he'll do next."

Her shoulders tightened. He could see her tears building. Unable to handle seeing her so upset, he eased her up and held her tight as she shook.

"I'll talk to Marcus, see if I can convince him to stay here."

"You know that won't work. This is personal. It's become all too personal," she murmured. Stepping back, she wiped her face as he frowned, refusing to let go. She sighed. "I never would've done any good in the service."

Gripping her hips, he squeezed. "Rashid is trying to throw us off balance, focusing on protection and safety instead of the company and the mole. We're either getting closer, or he's getting nervous for some reason."

Olivia winced as she raised her arms, pulling down her failing ponytail. A smile pushed onto his lips when her hair settled over her shoulders.

"I see that, but it still seems strange. Why come after you with only two men?" Her eyes looked to his as her hands rested on his arms. "If he knows you, he knows two men aren't enough."

He shrugged. "It's enough to distract me." With a heavy

breath, he released her and stepped back. A frown appeared on her face as she crossed her arms.

"There's a lot distracting me right now. I know you don't want me to say it, but please stay inside. I won't ask you to stay in your office, although it seems the safest place. But stay here. Don't go to your car or anywhere else outside the building."

She nodded, that frown fixed in place, but she didn't argue.

"Call Marcus if you need to leave. I'll see you later." He headed for her door.

"Promise."

Pausing, he grinned as he turned. Still staring him down, she smirked back.

"I'll see you later tonight. Don't leave."

She nodded, and he gently shut the door as a rush of adrenaline hit his body. He needed to find Coleston, find Rashid, and stop all this. And he needed to do it now.

Making his way to Marcus's floor, he knocked and opened the door, pausing at the sight of Marcus reloading his rifle.

"Planning on going hunting?"

Marcus snapped the barrel in place. "Possibly. You want to come along?"

He shook his head. "Your niece is worried about you. She thinks you'll go barreling into something and get yourself hurt."

"He was here in my building. I want him."

"Rashid?"

Marcus nodded and motioned Kenton around to the computer screen. A video file was paused, and when he started it, anger heated Kenton's face.

Rashid stood in the lobby. Hands in his pockets, he looked around, smiling at the cameras.

"He arrived right after the attack in the parking deck. It was a distraction. I'm done waiting. I've hired twenty-four-hour protection for Ollie, and when we leave today, she won't go anywhere without them until this is settled."

"I can't believe he was here." Straightening, Kenton paced the room, sick that Rashid had gotten so close to Olivia. "Marcus, you can't just go after him. You get that, right?"

"He was here. Olivia could've walked down to the lobby, and then what?"

He shook his head. "I get that. I do. Trust me, I'm just as mad. But this is different. Let me do my job. I need to find Coleston, and we need to give Bruno time to find something on Downing's computer."

Marcus sighed. "Tonight. You have until tonight. Then I'll be doing some hunting."

"Don't do anything until you talk to me. Deal?"

Marcus frowned but nodded. "Fine."

"Just think of Olivia. Don't do something that would hurt her."

"Perhaps you should be thinking that way as well, my friend."

Kenton glared a moment before giving him a nod. As he left the office, he pulled out his phone to find Bruno.

"What happened? I heard the sirens, and you haven't answered your cell."

"Rashid was in the building. I need you to reach out to federal, see if we can get some heat on him."

"Are you kidding? In the building?"

"Brune, come on." He sighed. "I'll get the still shot to you. If he is wanted for anything here, he'll be investigated. Maybe it will give us a reprieve. Where are you on the case? Have you found anything to get to Downing yet?"

"Not yet. I'll let you know."

"Hurry. This is getting out of hand."

Shoving the phone in his pocket, he pushed through to the stairwell. Mulling over Marcus's words, he gritted his teeth.

Marcus was right; he should be thinking much more about how he could potentially hurt Olivia.

After losing her family and having only Marcus left, she sure didn't need someone like him who couldn't hold on to a relationship for more than a few weeks. He would try his best, but really, didn't he always?

Walking into the parking garage, he frowned. Glaring at his decimated SUV, he sighed and called Bruno again.

"What now?"

"I need your car."

25

Olivia stared at her computer screen in frustration.

After going over the information on Rashid, the video feed from outside Marcus's office ran in the background. He was headed out to get Rashid on his own. It was only a matter of time. And watching the video was pointless. He could easily have some private entrance he hadn't even told her about.

With a sigh, she wiped her eyes and leaned against the desk. Kenton's cologne still lingered on her clothes, and she breathed in deeply before pulling up the email from Dawson.

The meeting for her possible reinstatement was set for Friday at nine in the morning. He'd assured her all her training over the past few years would provide enough experience, not to mention the IT degree she'd obtained since moving here. She just had to pass the physical.

Her heart sank as she pondered, rubbing her bottom lip with her finger. As much as she wanted to see her friends, to find some comfort in being home, it would end the same way. Alone and nameless in a crowd of faces, feeling as if whatever job she was working wasn't the goal.

She wasn't made for working with a team and a unit. Working alone was something she was proficient at and enjoyed. So, would going back, re-joining the military, even make her happy?

With a groan, she laid her head on the desk.

"What in the world am I supposed to do now, God? Where am I supposed to go?"

All the prayer, the scripture, never seemed to point in a specific direction. Wasn't that what God was supposed to do? Point her in the right direction? Then why did every single direction she followed end so abruptly?

Moving here had been the easiest decision she had made in her lifetime. Miserable and sad in her job, she missed Daniel, and everyone knew it. All the looks of pity simply made her more upset.

Daniel had been the love of her life. They'd fallen so quickly, easily, it had moved from friendship to something more as if it were meant to be within only a few weeks. It had been the only intimate relationship she'd ever experienced, and she'd planned on a lifetime with him.

Swallowing the hurt and memories, she let out a sigh. His death had left her alone with no one who understood what it meant to lose a loved one.

So Marcus offering her the opportunity to come here was the perfect escape.

Sitting up, she turned her phone end over end.

"Why here? Why come here and deal with all this? Why did this all happen after I showed up?"

Too many questions, not enough answers.

Her phone buzzed, and she answered. "Marcus?"

"Our protection is all lined up. Kenton has already agreed to drive you to the safe house tonight."

"Sounds wonderful," she muttered. "Are you behaving?"

A forced chuckle came over the line. "Of course."

"Then who are the men at your office door?"

Silence stretched for a moment as she watched the door to his office open and three men walk inside.

"I'm guessing you're watching surveillance videos for your own safety?"

"You mean for our safety."

"Right. Well, these men are some of my worker bees. I've got to go. I just want to make sure you know the plan for tonight. No going off alone, right?"

"I'll agree to it if you will."

His deep sigh made her chest ache. "Fine. See you tonight."

The call ended, and she set the phone down, shaking her head.

"God, please, please protect Marcus from himself."

"Why do you need to know?"

Olivia watched Mr. Downing shift under her gaze.

"I already talked to that other guy about all this."

"I know that, Mr. Downing, and I appreciate you meeting with me today."

"It's not like I had a choice."

She sat across from him, leaning back in her chair as his eyes narrowed. "You're an exceptional worker, but for some reason, you've been singled out as a man of controversy."

"That seems to be the consensus."

"The thing is, I'm trying to stop a cyberattack from the inside."

"Inside? I thought you guys said it was an outside attack?"

"The man responsible made it seem like he would be doing the dirty work, but I think our security is too strong. I think it has to be an inside job." She leaned into the table. "I also think someone is being paid a great deal to become a mole, to be used by this outsider."

Downing relaxed, his jaw loosening.

"I really don't think you have anything to do with it. However, I believe you have a viewpoint several that work here do not."

"And what is that?"

"You don't have loyalties, Mr. Downing."

"Loyalties?"

"I can ask you any question, and you'll give me a straight answer because you don't owe anyone anything."

He smiled crookedly. "What is it you think I can tell you?"

"Who from inside this company would be willing to sell out?"

His jaw tightened again. "I don't know."

"Oh, come now, Mr. Downing. I can tell you find yourself alone at the top, so to speak, when it comes to intelligence. So tell me who would sabotage this company for financial gain, and we'll be able to move past all this."

"I don't know." He let out a long sigh. "I don't know many people here, but so far, most are just ants. They come to work, do their measly little jobs, and go home. They have no ambition or desire to create. I have no use for getting to know them, so no, I have no idea who would attack from inside the company."

Although he appeared to be telling the truth, he was holding back.

"Very well. You can go back to your station."

Watching Mr. Downing leave, her gut churned. He knew Coleston well and still didn't out him as a possible risk. That meant they were in it together, or Coleston really did have Downing tricked.

She needed a confession if they were going to get to Coleston. And she was running out of time.

26

———

After spending two hours watching Coleston, Kenton was relieved by another officer.

"Just let me know if anything changes."

The officer nodded, and Kenton took off back to the Institute.

So far, according to Bruno, Coleston hadn't made a move to get in touch with Rashid. But then again, Coleston had tech skills and gadgets. There was no telling what was going on inside that house.

With a sigh, he pulled into the garage and stepped out of the SUV as Marcus exited the elevator, three men in tow.

"I thought we had a deal?" Kenton frowned as Marcus gave him that glare.

"Wait for me." Marcus nodded to the men, sending them to several black, unmarked vehicles.

"Marcus."

"Before you overreact, I have eyes and ears open. There's been some chatter, and I'm simply following up. The men are for protection. I'm not going into this thing alone."

"I thought you weren't going in at all. At least not until I let you know what I found."

"And what have you found?"

He shook his head.

"I want to know where he is, and I want eyes on him at all times. He won't step foot in my building or one of my homes again without consequences."

"So you're going in to observe?"

Marcus's eyes narrowed. "No hunting allowed. I've been warned by my niece. She'll do her part if I do mine."

At least that was something.

"I've already put protection in place. These three are part of that. When we finish, we'll head to the house. You receive the address?"

"Earlier. I'll get her there safely."

"And you'll stay until I arrive?"

He nodded. "Of course."

Marcus's jaw tightened as he nodded back. "Then I'll see you tonight."

"Stay safe."

Without a word, Marcus slid inside the open door of the SUV, and the group drove away.

Shaking his head, Kenton stepped into the elevator and headed upstairs.

Walking into the break room they were using, he grabbed a bottle of water and sat down at the computer. Pulling up the Institute's website, he searched through the recent technological advances.

His phone vibrated.

"Matthews."

"Detective Matthews?"

"Yes, who's this?"

"This is Senior Agent McMurray. Agent Billings is my agent."

"Yes. We met the other day."

"I wanted to let you know he was in the wrong."

Kenton leaned into the table.

"In our business, we're not careful enough. After what happened, I'd like to discuss a possible job opening."

"A job? You want to offer me a job after what happened with Billings?"

"I want you to consider that your experience is an asset, not something to be hidden with assessments."

He tensed. "And what experience is that?"

"After what happened, I did some digging. We could use someone with your talents."

"I'm not looking for a career change. But if you have something on that bomb, that would be helpful."

A deep sigh echoed over the phone. "Your boss told me you probably wouldn't go for it."

Kenton smiled. "He's right. The bomb?"

"It was homemade with no signature. Nothing to lead us to a maker."

"The car?"

"Plates came back stolen from a lot in a county north of here. It was a small lot with few cameras. We didn't get anything more than a grainy figure. The video from the car entering downtown and parking was a better picture, but the man who exited wore a hoodie and dark sunglasses. No way to ID."

"I want both videos."

"Sure, you can take a look. It's not going to change anything."

As they exchanged emails, Kenton stood from the table.

"One more thing, Matthews."

"Yeah?"

"Who do you think is behind it? Three of my men were

injured and one is in the ICU, might not make it out. I'd like to find who did it."

"Not at liberty to discuss it. Besides, I have no proof."

"Someone like you might not need proof."

"Some like me, huh?" Shaking his head, he let out a sigh. "Sorry, can't give you anything. If I find something, you'll be the first call I make."

"Thanks. You can call anytime. You have a change of heart, let me know."

"Thanks." Kenton hung up, his phone beeping at an incoming email.

"Hey, what's up?" Bruno came inside and sat down.

"I'm sending you a couple of videos. One is of the lot they stole the SUV from, and the other shows after it was parked downtown. I want you to take a look."

Bruno pulled up the video as Kenton sat again.

"Man, talk about grainy. I'm not going to be able to clear this up."

The video ran black and white with a nondescript man walking across the lot and using a Slim Jim to open the late model SUV. He slid in and the car disappeared.

"Where did he come from?"

"There's a lot here." Bruno rewound the video. "Here's something."

A dark truck pulled up at the curb on the far side of the lot. The person exited, and a logo was visible on the truck door, disappearing as the door closed.

"Can you get that image fixed?"

Bruno winced. "If I can run it through what they have here, yeah, I can probably figure it out. Let me talk to Drone and see what he says."

Kenton nodded. If they could trace the car that had dropped off the man who stole the SUV, they would have a lead. One that might take them to the bomber and, hopefully, Rashid.

27

"You're saying this isn't you?"

Kenton leaned on the table, glaring down the man they'd quickly ID'd and picked up as the driver of the stolen SUV. Arthur Gerod. The Institute's technology for facial recognition was better than anything he'd seen.

"You've got a grainy image, nothing concrete. If you had evidence I was in that car, I'd be under arrest."

"We've got the truck you got out of and an ATM camera that puts you, not just the truck, at that lot the night this SUV was stolen." He sat down and pulled the pictures from the file. "I can place you here, taking this car, and then this happened." He shoved the pictures of the exploded vehicle toward Arthur. "A bombing that put three members of the bomb squad in the hospital. With your record, that's probable cause."

"What?" Arthur stood. "You've got to be kidding me. You've got nothing."

"My boss says the DA is willing to go along with it. Sit down." Kenton leaned back as Arthur sat. "You see, it destroyed a lot of property, put three of our own in the hospital, and injured several more bystanders. The public wants justice. And since you're the only one we've got on video, it's probable cause to look through your bank records, your home."

"What? You went through my home?" Arthur paled as he held his head in his hands. "Look, it was a job. An easy job."

"Who paid?"

"Some guy. I didn't ask questions." Arthur looked up. "I swear, I have no idea who they are or what they do. I just help out when I need money. Whatever they do with the cars, that's on them."

"Cars? As in plural? How many?"

Arthur started to shake.

"I don't care about this." Kenton pointed at the pictures. "I want to know who paid you and what other cars you took."

"I get another strike, I'm done."

"You've already got it, man. Do yourself some good."

Arthur groaned. "I don't meet anyone. I just get a package delivered with instructions and some cash. I follow the instructions."

"Other cars?"

"Usually late model vans, passenger movers, things like that."

Kenton stood. "He's all yours."

"Wait. I thought you were going to help me?"

"Not me."

The door opened, and Detective Anders entered. "Well?"

Kenton tossed the file on his desk as he looked at Captain Post. "That logo is part of some kind of monopoly, Bruno's not been able to crack it yet. But it doesn't give us a name."

"You mean the name you're hoping for? Is it the same person you think is trying to hack the Institute?"

Kenton shrugged. "I want to think it's the same. But even if it isn't, those bomb squad members deserve an answer for why that bomb was there."

"I was under the impression it was because of you."

"No proof yet. But if there is any, Anders will figure it out." He glanced at his phone. "I've got to go."

"How's the case at the Institute going?"

"It's not. All appearances indicate it's impossible to hack into their systems, but we have a deadline. So we'll be there to keep it as safe as possible."

Post frowned. "That doesn't sound promising."

"Honestly, we need more. More help and more access. The board members have one of their own who is a person of interest, but we can't touch him. They won't approve Bruno to get into his system to determine if he's the mole or not."

"Be sure to put that in your report. This company has a lot of pull. I want it on record that we did our jobs regardless of what they didn't allow us to do."

He nodded and headed out of the office and to his car.

Olivia leaned against the windowsill as Bruno went over the video again.

"If you didn't see anything the first dozen times, I have a hard time believing you'll see something this time."

Bruno shrugged. "That's the job. If this leads us to the bomber, who is either Rashid or hired by Rashid, we've got something to go after him with."

Kenton walked in, pausing as a smile spread across his face, his gaze locking with hers.

"You get him?"

Kenton turned to Bruno and took a seat. "No luck. He was hired by a faceless agent who gave him cash and instructions. No names, no way to trace. Detective Anders will cinch it up. Let me know if there's anything that tracks."

"The company logo, what was it?" She walked up behind Bruno to look over the logo on the laptop screen.

"It's for a company called MetMed Pack. It's some investment conglomerate. But there's nothing there leading to an actual person. It's all online with automated services. There's no name associated with the Better Business Bureau or even with the state."

"So, a shell corporation?"

Kenton nodded as he glanced at her. "A perfect way for someone like Rashid to hide his presence in the States."

"Did you send this to Marcus?"

Kenton stood. "Yes."

"By the way, I've turned in the still of Rashid."

"What? What're you talking about?"

Bruno grimaced.

She turned her attention to Kenton, who was staring at his partner. "What is he talking about?"

"During the shootout earlier, Rashid entered the building."

"What?" Face heating, her hands fisted. "What did he do?"

"He just stood there, looking at the cameras. He wanted us to know he was here. But now that we have the face of a possible terrorist in the US, I'm hoping the feds will take notice."

"What if they start asking questions?"

Kenton didn't even look at Bruno. "If they do, we give them what we have. I'm hopeful he'll realize he's made a mistake and will back off. But right now, we need to get to the safe house."

"Where's Marcus?"

"I saw him leave with a detail of three men. He's not going after anything other than information. But he's smart enough to take protection with him."

Sure. *Protection.*

"Brune, let me know if you figure anything else out."

"Will do."

Kenton's arm went around her waist and turned her,

escorting her to the door. "Let's get your things and go to the safe house."

She entered the elevator in silence. As they slid into the SUV several minutes later, Kenton assured her, "He's going to be fine."

"You don't know him as well as I do."

He chuckled as they left the garage. "I think I know him well enough to understand how angry he is and what he's willing to do to protect you. But I also know he's too smart and doesn't like to lose. If he's going to go after Rashid, he'll do it with the best men he can find."

"You won't be there."

A muscle jumped in his jaw as he checked his mirrors. "He trusts me with something much more important."

Heart pounding, she clasped her hands together on her lap. With all the hugging, his hands holding her arms, her back, leading and guiding her all over the place, her mind was wandering much too far.

Although, to be fair, Kenton was a hard man to refuse. Her girlfriends would have a fit if they knew just how hard she was pushing him away.

Well, not really that hard.

"Want to talk about it?"

"Talk about what?"

"Whatever put that smile on your face."

"I wasn't smiling."

He chuckled.

Leaning against the door, she checked the mirror.

"No one is following. I promise."

"I trust you."

"That's good to know."

"You think after all this I don't?"

He shrugged, a smirk on his lips.

"Kenton, remember how I stayed with you so willingly?"

"*Willingly?* I'm not sure you're using the right word, Olivia."

She chuckled. "I can assure you, that was willingly. I never would've stayed with anyone I didn't fully trust."

He licked his lips, jaw still tight as he watched the mirrors.

"Nothing to add?"

"No, not a thing."

Leaning back to watch her mirror, she tried to avoid the thought of staying at his home, waking up to see that smile of his, bare-chested and ... *don't go there.*

Sighing, she pushed the thoughts from her mind to prepare for another night with Kenton, Marcus, and her new protection detail.

Between Marcus hunting down Rashid, her future up in the air, and Rashid walking into their building, worry filled her mind.

Why was he there? To distract them? To threaten her?

Heart pounding, she took a deep breath. Then there was Kenton.

What was she going to do about him?

28

———————

Oliva walked into the living room, frowning at the fact she appeared to be all alone.

She'd locked herself in her room after Kenton did a quick and quiet inspection before allowing her inside. After changing and unpacking her bags, it was odd he'd not knocked on her door or been waiting when she came out.

Maybe not odd. Maybe she was just hopeful.

Lord, give me some grace, please.

There was no way he left, not after promising he'd stay until Marcus arrived with his replacements. Looking out the back window, she saw Kenton pacing the back deck and unlocked the door to join him.

"What're you doing?"

"I was going to ask you the same thing. Why aren't you inside?" Wrapping her arms around her body, she watched as Kenton tilted his head.

"I'm doing my job. With everyone finding us and all the attacks, I'm not interested in taking chances. You need to get inside."

She rolled her eyes and paced toward the edge of the deck, rotating her neck and shaking off the day's stress.

"Olivia."

"Why do you always call me that?"

"It's starting to get dark. I think you need to go inside."

Shaking her head, she studied the large grassy area at the back of the house, the fence separating the other properties. The cool breeze moved in, making her shiver. Kenton was suddenly behind her, his hands moving up and down her arms, carefully avoiding her stitches.

Leaning back, she closed her eyes and smiled at how easy it was to feel at ease and rest when he was around. His arms wrapped around her middle, his breath on her neck gave her goosebumps.

"Why don't you go inside," he whispered, and her whole body shivered.

Taking a breath, she nodded. "Yeah, I think I should." Clearing her throat, she stepped around him.

He held her arm and she refrained from letting him pull her in. Looking up at his blue eyes, she narrowed her focus, trying to figure out why he kept pulling her in only to let her go so easily.

"Something on your mind?" A smirk graced his lips.

"Trying to figure out what's on yours."

He chuckled, letting his hand drop down to hold hers. "It's been a busy few days."

She frowned. "Busy, yes, but I—"

"Olivia." He sighed, breaking eye contact to scan the yard. "You really need to get inside."

She crossed her arms, watching his smirk disappear.

"Don't look at me like that."

"When are your replacements coming?"

"Marcus said by eleven." He shifted his gaze back and forth from her to the yard.

"Then what?"

He sighed. "You'll be safe inside, and I'll stay outside in the car."

"In the car? What's the point of having a group here to protect us if you're going to sit alone in your car?" She held her hips and glared. "You've talked so much about me getting rest, but you need some too."

"I'm good."

"So, you won't go home or stay inside, but you'll sit outside? I don't understand."

"That's what I need to do."

With a shake of her head, she turned to the door.

"Olivia."

"Look." She turned to face him, working to ease the emotions building up after the past few days. "I don't understand what's going on here, but you keep pushing and then pulling. Don't wrap me up, then tell me to leave, then take my hand."

He frowned and stepped into her space, shoving his hands in his pockets. "You're distracting."

She thought he was kidding, but his face showed no humor.

"I can't do this job if you're distracting me like this. I need to protect you. That's my job, and you make that difficult."

Her eyes searched his, working to form a sentence. "But I'm the one trying to leave, and then you—"

He groaned and edged closer, grabbing her hand. "I can't just not reach out to you, but I have to focus, and you make that hard."

Seeing those blue eyes darken, staring into hers as he squeezed her hand, she wondered how she was going to leave without falling apart.

"Keeping you safe is all that matters right now. Do you understand?" He broke eye contact as he searched behind her, body tense.

"I'm going inside," she whispered.

"Just try and understand, okay?"

"Then stop pushing." She pulled her hand away, her heart pounding. "I realize you think I play games, but I don't. My heart doesn't work that way. I've lost too much to love and let go as if it were nothing. Just stop pushing. Stop keeping me from leaving."

He frowned, giving her a slight nod before she turned and hurried inside. Rushing to the bedroom, she slammed the door, collapsing on the bed and finally letting go. Her body ached, her arm burned, and now, her heart hurt.

She had started to depend on him too much. She wanted him with her to give her comfort and that sense of safety. As much as she understood what he was saying, she didn't understand why he didn't want to stay inside tonight, to stay here with her. The protection Marcus hired would be the best, but there was no reason Kenton shouldn't want to stay.

Taking a breath, she wiped her face and sat up. Sitting around crying over a man she didn't understand, a situation she couldn't control, wasn't her norm. Besides, it would be best if he left. She'd be leaving soon herself and would need to get used to his absence.

With a sigh, she headed to the bathroom and started a bath, needing something relaxing to help her rest tonight. Because now, Marcus wasn't the only one she was terrified of losing.

29

"Great job, man," Kenton mumbled, walking toward the side of the house.

He thought putting the situation out there, making a point to tell her he was no longer playing, that there was something more, would help. Only now, he had made things worse. That little bit of focus he had was fading away.

That was terrifying.

Pausing in his walk, he exhaled and closed his eyes. In his entire life, he had been terrified only a few times. When his mother was sick with cancer and passed away, his very first tour in the service, and the day he thought he was dead. Those three times in his life, he was truly scared.

But living in fear for Olivia was different. It hit him hard. His insides ached, and his stomach clenched at the thought of anything happening to her.

As the evening wore on, he did his best to keep out of the house. Being inside with her was impossible. She didn't seem to understand that as much as he reached out to her, she came to him just as easily.

She had searched him out, came to him every time, and he loved it, craved it. For the first time in his life, he had someone who cared where he was and what he was doing. Someone who wanted to be there for him.

Pacing the front porch, he halted as Marcus's BMW pulled into the drive, a black SUV behind him. Marcus got out and headed his way, searching the outside of the house.

"Banished to the porch, huh?" Marcus looked him over with a smirk.

"Just keeping an eye out."

Marcus nodded, then motioned to the men following him. "This is Bryant and his team. They are held in high esteem, and after our discussion, we will be dutifully protected."

He nodded to the four-man team as they headed inside.

"So, where is she?"

"Inside." Kenton started off the porch when Marcus called to him.

"Where're you going?"

He turned. "Home. You've got a good team. I've heard of them. They're the best."

"So, you're just leaving? Like that?" Marcus crossed his arms with a frown.

"Did you have something you wanted to discuss?"

Marcus shook his head. "No, not really. Did you say anything to Ollie?"

He frowned. "We talked. She's expecting you. Just call me if something comes up." He left before Marcus inquired more about Olivia.

Sliding into the SUV, he started it up and glanced at the house. Even with the curtains and shades drawn, he could see the lights burning in the windows. He noticed the shade moving at her room and sighed.

"She's right. I need sleep." He tried to find something to make himself feel better about leaving without saying goodbye.

He would see her tomorrow. Maybe she'd be in a better mood then. Gripping the wheel, he grunted and pulled away, making himself put the house behind him. The ache in his chest tightened, his breath straining.

"Breathe, just breathe. She'll be safe. God, let her be safe."

30

—————

Sunday Morning

Kenton groaned and rolled from the bed, rubbing his eyes and yawning. It had been a long night of tossing and turning, regretting his decision not to say goodbye to Olivia and hating leaving things the way they were. His worry for her safety urged him awake, but he had reassured himself all night that she was safe with the detail Marcus had hired.

"God, give me something here," he mumbled as he went to shower.

Cleaner and more awake, he sat in his kitchen, remembering her sitting here at breakfast the day before. It seemed more than natural for her to be here, curled up on his couch and sitting with him as they ate breakfast.

He missed her desperately.

Pulling out his phone, he hoped for a peace offering once again.

Sleep well?

Of course not.

He sighed.

Sorry, Olivia.

He waited, but no other messages came through.

"Way to mess it all up, man."

As he walked into the Institute around eight, he headed toward the stairwell once again to find Bruno.

His heart in his throat, he pushed through to see his partner leaning against the table, head in his hand, his hair a mess and in the same clothes as yesterday.

"You find anything?"

Bruno turned with a grin. "I've got him."

"Him who?"

"What's wrong? You look awful."

"Brune, just tell me what you've got."

"I've got Downing. I tried a backdoor, figuring it wouldn't lead to anything, seeing as how he's a pro. But I found a trail, a link online with similar coding to the hack. I've been comparing the two, sent it to Drone to double check."

He sighed. "So, we have the hack but not the man. We don't even have Coleston."

Bruno shook his head. "Not yet, but this seems to link up."

"We need to tell Marcus. Come on." With a deep breath, he stood and led Bruno to Marcus's office. Pushing through the door, that lump in his throat returned as he saw Olivia standing beside Marcus. Beautiful as always. Her jaw was taut as they locked eyes.

"Kenton?"

Pulling his gaze from Olivia, he nodded at Marcus. "I think we have something. Tell 'em, Brune."

"So, what? You're done?" Olivia stared.

Kenton's jaw ached as he clenched it tightly, trying to find something else to say. Bruno breaking everything down seemed to tie it all up neatly. If only they had something on Rashid.

"I'll go see where Drone is on the comparison." Bruno nodded to him and left.

"We have our hacker, and Bruno will monitor the system tonight. I plan on interrogating Downing, see if he can give me something. If he confesses, I'll no longer be assigned to the case." He looked past Olivia to Marcus. "That being said, you know I'm in this. I don't have to be here because I'm ordered to. That's not why I came in the first place."

Marcus nodded. "I appreciate that." He sighed and stood. "I'm trying to figure out how to get ahold of Coleston. The board isn't convinced."

Kenton focused on Olivia as she paced and turned away from him.

Pushing his gaze to Marcus, he shoved his hands in his pockets. "If we can get Downing to see that Coleston was messing with his computer, we might get an idea of what Coleston is up to."

"That won't happen."

"Why not?"

Olivia shrugged. "He won't give us anything on Coleston unless we have proof."

Kenton crossed his arms. "Why is that?"

"I spoke with him yesterday." She locked eyes with him. "He's a narcissist and believes he's above everyone here. I gave him every opportunity to throw Coleston under the bus, and he never mentioned him. Either he really doesn't know Coleston's plan, or he thinks Coleston has his back."

"All that from one conversation?"

She nodded. "But the main problem is Rashid. How're we going to track him?"

"I'm not convinced we can. But he won't quit."

Marcus leaned against his desk. "There's always a way to find him out."

"No." Olivia shook her head, her jaw clenched.

"We need evidence, a connection. Bruno doesn't have anything that connects them. If it were there, he would find it."

Marcus frowned.

"Coleston is too smart for that. You'll never connect them. You'll have to get a confession first." Olivia barely glanced at him, her focus on Marcus.

"If Rashid's where I think he is, we can find evidence."

Kenton shook his head. "Not legally."

"After coming for Olivia, I don't need legality on my side." Marcus hissed.

Kenton groaned and stood. "I can't hear that." He paced a moment. "I'm not going to let you do something stupid."

"I don't need your permission," Marcus smirked.

"So, this is funny to you?"

Kenton sighed as Olivia looked ready to go off on them both.

"Love, this isn't what you think." Marcus tried to approach her but stopped short as her hand went up. "Neither of us considers this case solved. We both understand how all this works, much better than you know. With Rashid loose, I'm still concerned for you."

"For me? You're the one he wants, not me."

"He knows how important you are to me."

She frowned.

"Olivia, he'll do whatever it takes to get to Marcus," Kenton offered.

She ignored him as she brushed past, fisting her hands and pushing out the door.

"Well, that went well," Kenton muttered.

Marcus sat down, patting the chair next to him. Kenton collapsed with a sigh.

"I assume things aren't going well?"

He looked over with a frown. "What things?"

"Oh, come on, Kenton. I'm not blind. Much more is happening between the two of you than either of you wants to admit. As much as I don't think you worthy of her, you're about the only man I'd ever consider safe for her."

Kenton's face heated as he leaned in on his knees.

"I see a change in her."

"You mean the anger? Irritation? Frustration?"

Marcus chuckled as he slapped his shoulder. "She's fighting it as much as you are, I think."

"Marcus, you assume too much. Attraction is great. She's a beautiful and intelligent woman. But I'm not ... you know enough to understand I'm not the right man."

"I'll never understand why you think yourself so unworthy. We've had this discussion before. You need to see that God thinks so much more of you."

Kenton shook his head. "Marcus, I can't make her happy. Not happy enough to want to stay here."

That was the plain truth. Olivia was an amazing woman, and as infatuated as he found himself with her, the more he thought about it, the more he realized she needed much more than he could give.

"I think it's all adding up. God's put us together for this reason. She's not keen on meeting new people, opening herself up to anyone. The fear they'll leave. I think that's what she's held on to since childhood."

Marcus sighed. "I never promised to come home. I was terrified I would ruin her if I ever broke that promise. I know she's lonely. She's missing the comfort of home. She has no friends here. No one she's confided in."

"How do you know?"

"She's not the happy girl I knew years ago."

"What made her happy?"

Marcus sat back. "I'd been home for a few years, spending time with her and trying to keep from getting too anxious." He chuckled. "I met a few of her friends, the same girls she had known for years. I think she was dating someone. I interrupted a few phone calls here and there, but I could never find out more. She kept things to herself."

He chuckled. "Like her uncle."

"Yes. But after a few months, she finally told me she had been dating a good friend. One she had met while in the protection service. I met him once. He seemed nervous, a good sign."

Kenton laughed.

"But right before I accepted this job, he was killed in the line of duty. It devastated her. Ever since, she's not been the happy, smiling, wonderful woman I had known all her life. She stopped going out with her friends, being social.

"I made it here and, after a year, convinced her to come work with me. She agreed, which surprised me. I didn't think she'd come." Marcus leaned next to him. "Kenton, I want my happy girl back."

Kenton nodded. "I'm not sure I'm the man for the job."

Marcus stood. "If you continue to sit here with me, you won't be." He winked.

"Marcus."

"Go."

He slowly stood with a grunt and nodded. "If she's planning on going back"—he swallowed at the lump in his throat—"no promises."

Marcus nodded.

Taking his time walking to the elevator, Kenton took a deep

breath. Olivia seemed even more upset with him today than when he'd left last night. He should've stayed.

Staring out her window, Olivia couldn't find any peace. Dark rain clouds filled the sky as she leaned her forehead against the window and closed her eyes.

Hearing that Kenton was done and that Marcus was determined to go after Rashid made her heart ache. Kenton would do anything to protect Marcus, and Marcus would do anything for her. They would go after Rashid no matter the cost.

"Lord, give them some kind of protection. Or sound minds."

A chuckle made her spin with a start. Kenton leaned against her desk.

"What? Why're you here?"

"Marcus told me to come."

She frowned. Like that was the answer she wanted to hear. But after last night, what did she expect?

"Oh, he did? Well, you can tell him I'm otherwise occupied." Hurrying to her desk, she fell into her chair and pulled herself up to the computer.

"Olivia, are you mad at me?"

She opened her email and attempted to divert her attention. "I'm busy. My company is at risk, and I'm head of security. Imagine what will happen if we're breached again."

Kenton stepped beside her, leaning against the desk and pushing into her chair. "That doesn't answer my question."

Forcing her lips closed, she held back the torrent of words she wanted to let loose.

"You know, Marcus told me you used to have a great group of friends back home."

She shook her head and went back to typing.

"Have you considered going home for a visit?"

"Really? A vacation? You think that's on my mind right now?" She met his smirk with a glare. "You have some nerve."

"So you are mad at me?"

Slamming her hand down on the desk, she pushed away and stood, gripping her hips to keep from lashing out. "Allowing Marcus to entertain the idea of going after Rashid as if it's some game. What're you thinking?"

Kenton's jaw tensed as he stared at her in silence.

"You act as if you need to find a way out of all this, and then you find your way back in as if it's nothing."

"I've never looked for a way out of this. Marcus is the closest friend I have. I wouldn't back away when he needs help."

She scoffed. "You said the other night—"

He stood, pushing into her space. "When I'm on duty, when I'm trying to do my job and protect you, I have to find a way to make space. Right now, we're someplace safer, someplace where I don't have to be on constant alert. This is different."

Crossing her arms, she leaned against the wall and glared. It seemed they were at a stalemate once again.

"I'm sorry I left last night without coming in." His jaw clenched. "I'm trying here. Trying to figure all this out."

Her eyes narrowed. "Figure out what?"

"As much as I would like to think this could be much, much more, I don't know if I can or even if you would want more. Marcus has his hopes up."

She frowned.

Kenton took hold of her elbows, stepping closer. "I want to stay and finish this, find a way to get to Rashid. Is that something you can handle?"

"Why are you asking me?"

"I want your opinion. If you don't want me here—"

"You'll leave?" She raised her eyebrow as he frowned.

"If you don't want me here, I'll speak with Marcus. I can help and keep my distance."

"That's up to Marcus."

His blue eyes searched hers. "Why did you come to the US?"

Her heart tightened. "That's personal."

"Want to share?"

She shook her head. He leaned down to her ear.

"Olivia, I'm sorry you've dealt with so much. But I can promise you, I'm not going anywhere unless you ask me to."

His breath sent a shiver through her body. "I assume Marcus has been telling stories."

"No, he's worried about you. He says you're not happy anymore, and for some reason, he thinks I can help."

She huffed, making him chuckle. With a sigh, she leaned into his chest, letting him take her weight as he held her up.

"I'm worried about Marcus. I can't lose him too. This is just too close to home, and I don't know how to handle it. When he was overseas, I could pretend, ignore the danger he was in. But here, I can't deal with all this."

Kenton gave her a squeeze. "He loves you. He wants to protect you. If you think I haven't considered going after Rashid as well, you'd be wrong."

That comment seemed to contain more than she'd expected. Sliding her hands around his waist, she leaned in and felt the rumble through his chest as he spoke.

"I'm staying. I'm not going anywhere until I know you're safe. And I'd like to find a way to make you smile again. You have an amazing smile."

She sighed, feeling much more moving between them once again. "I'm wondering if you're here simply because Marcus wanted you to come."

He chuckled and leaned back, pulling her chin up to see

him. "I might have his blessing to come find you, but no, that's not why I'm here. You should see that by now."

Her face heating, she nodded.

"So, until you tell me not to, I'll be here helping to finish this all up."

"Still being protective, I guess."

His eyes searched hers. "Trust me, I'm not getting too far. I ..." He breathed out, his lips pursing.

"What?"

A red rush washed across his cheeks. "I am sorry about not coming to see you last night."

"I think you have something else to say."

He chuckled. "Not at the moment."

She frowned, unwilling to break eye contact. Although, it didn't seem to bother him.

"What do you have planned for today?"

He sidestepped the comment and her, letting go and shoving his hands in his pockets. Why couldn't he just say whatever was on his mind?

With a sigh and shake of her head, she returned to her desk, working to ease the irritation. He had been through a lot too. With his injury and sleeplessness, he had to be exhausted. That should be enough for her to go easy on him.

But she didn't want to.

"Now I think there's something else on your mind."

She shrugged, focusing on the computer screen and her emails again. "I thought you had an interrogation to perform?"

He chuckled. "I'm waiting on Bruno's confirmation of what he found on the computer. Then, with a little luck, maybe I can get more on Coleston or Rashid."

"Then you better get to it," she said, too irritated to play any games today.

The pressure on the back of her chair made her recline as Kenton leaned in.

"Is this where you'll be today?"

She nodded, working to move her chair back to the desk as he stood behind her.

"Then this is where I expect to find you when I get back. Please don't leave. This is far from over."

His breath on her neck from behind made her shiver.

"I have too much work to do to be running around."

"Good."

A kiss brushed the side of her head, the chair returned to normal as she watched him walk out of her office.

Blowing out a sigh, she held her head in her hand as she leaned an elbow on the desk.

"Lord, please give me something here. I need a great deal of grace to make it through all this."

31

S miling, Kenton made his way downstairs to the room where Alonso Downing waited. Bruno had been right; the email found on Downing's computer had the same coding as the first email sent to Marcus about the upcoming attack.

"We've got enough to prosecute him." Bruno grinned as Kenton took the file, both the email from Downing and the email to Marcus printed out in front of him.

"Good, let's see what we can stir up."

In the interrogation room, he sat across from Downing.

"Why am I here again? Between you and that woman, I don't have anything else to tell you."

The man's face was red again, his arms crossed as his whole body tensed. The possibility of getting anything more from him seemed to be disappearing rapidly.

"We have something."

Kenton took Bruno's arm, silencing him. Leaning back in his chair, he crossed his arms and eased his irritation.

"Mr. Downing, I'd like to know what it would take for you to destroy this company."

Downing smirked. "What? I already told you. I've done nothing wrong."

"Okay, so what did it take for you to destroy the previous company you worked for?"

Downing's smirk vanished.

"We were told you were fired for trying to steal information."

"What? I don't need to steal any information. Those people were morons, all of them. No security protocols, no protection. I was just showing them the fault of their ways."

Kenton chuckled. "Just proving the intelligent wrong, huh? Sounds like a good day."

Bruno huffed.

"So, why come work here? From what I've been told, the smartest people in the world work here. How can you prove them wrong?"

"First of all, most of these so-called intelligent workers are drones. They perform the same tasks over and over with no imagination, no stepping up and looking for something new. They have nothing to offer this company. I have the talent and foresight to know what can make this company work."

"So, what would it take for you to destroy this company?"

Downing shrugged. "Money is always a plus. But I plan on making a lot of money here. I have ideas that need technology. This company is the only place that has what I need. So what? You're going to fire me because of what happened at that other place? They were the morons, not me."

Kenton chuckled. "Actually, we're going to charge you with trade secret theft."

Downing's mouth dropped. "What? I just told you I don't need to steal anything from here. I need the tech to make my ideas work."

"What if I said I believe you?"

Downing leaned in. "Why would you?"

"I think there's someone else trying to do damage. But I have no proof. I'm willing to believe you're a scapegoat."

"I'm not anyone's scapegoat. I'm too smart for them to use me like that." Downing narrowed his eyes as he tapped his finger on the tabletop.

"Who here would do that? Who here would consider themselves smarter than you, thinking they could use you and destroy the company at the same time?"

"There's no one here smarter—" Downing paused, his eyes widening. "That Coleston."

"You mean the head of the department Coleston? The man that's devoted his life to this company?" Kenton shook his head. "You'll have to do better than that, man."

"No, you don't understand." Downing leaned back. "He's a real piece of work. Granted, he's intelligent. Most of the tech began as an idea, and he was able to create it through this company. But that's all the credit I'll give him."

"I'm going to need more." Kenton's patience started to wear thin.

Downing sighed. "Look, I've uploaded a program on my computer that monitors clicks and passcodes. I use it to make sure my computer isn't tampered with."

He glanced at Bruno, who nodded.

"On my second day, after the breach, I did my usual sweep and found someone had been using my unit. The coding was impressive. I knew it had to be Coleston. But because of the attack, I didn't have a way to confront him. The last thing I wanted was to be seen arguing or making a scene when everyone was looking for whoever hacked the system."

"Was your computer the hack? Did someone set it up?" Bruno leaned in.

Downing shook his head. "Nope. I did a scan and found my email had been hacked. A few things were moved around, but I never figured out what was happening or what they took. I had nothing of importance in any of it, nothing illegal or anything.

"But then, when I tried to dig deeper, you guys showed up and confiscated my system before I could finish running my diagnostics. Whatever you found that you think links me to the hack, it wasn't mine. Someone put it there."

Kenton looked over at Bruno.

"It's possible. It was an email that was embedded. That could be what he was planting."

"You know who did it?"

Kenton turned his attention back across the table. "Mr. Downing, you understand that your being at this institute with false credentials looks deceiving right?"

Downing frowned.

"Then, of course, you just implicated your boss, Mr. Coleston, when we have several videos of you having what appears to be personal conversations."

"Yeah, we talked. He seemed to understand where I was coming from. That I wanted more than to code and go over systems analytics. He was interested in my ideas, said he would do what he could to get me in a better position to develop tech."

Kenton nodded as he stood. "You'll be escorted to the station where you will be booked and charged. You can call your lawyer from there."

"But you just said you know who put the email there."

He shrugged and headed for the door. "It's on your system, and we don't have proof that the person seen at your computer actually put the email there. Between that and the nature of your false acceptance into the company, you're going to be charged. I can't help that."

Slamming the door on Downing's tirade, Kenton blew out a breath.

"That went well. I wonder if it's enough for the board to let us into Coleston's system."

Kenton shrugged. "Even if it is, the guy's had a few days to clean it up. If there was any evidence on it, he wouldn't leave it sitting around for us to find."

"But he's been out of the office, placed on leave. He's not had access to his system."

"Then how does Marcus have access to his system from home? If you think someone like Coleston doesn't have protocols in place, you aren't thinking straight."

Bruno frowned. "I want a chance to look into it. If there's even the slightest possibility I can get to Rashid, I want to try."

He nodded. "Let's see what Marcus has to say."

32

───────

Hours later, Kenton paced Marcus's office as the sound of Bruno typing away on his computer echoed in the silent room.

"It's a no-go."

He turned to see Marcus enter, Olivia trailing behind him with a red face.

"What? How on earth?"

Marcus held up his hand to Bruno. "The board saw the video of the interrogation, and they do believe there is something there. But as I told you, Coleston has stock. He can't just be ousted, and nothing short of a confession or hard evidence will be enough to investigate. The board saw an ill-tempered, narcissistic man who lied about hacking the system."

Kenton's jaw clenched as he watched Olivia pacing in the background. "So what happens if the hack goes as planned?"

"Well, I imagine I'll be out of a job." Olivia glared at him for a moment before continuing her pacing.

"We might both be," Marcus said. "But that's not what I want to discuss. About Rashid."

"Bruno, take a walk." Kenton nodded at Bruno.

"Yeah, I'll go meet up with Drone, see what else we can do about protection for tonight."

As the door slammed shut, Kenton turned to Marcus. "I don't want him involved. He doesn't understand off book, and if he gets wind of even the slightest thing straying outside the law, he won't handle it well."

Marcus nodded. "Understood. But I do have information on Rashid. I received an email from a friend verifying his location."

"But what good does that do us? Rashid can't be connected to what's happening here. We have nothing to prosecute him with." Olivia's voice rose a notch.

Kenton leaned a hip against the desk as Marcus collapsed in the chair.

"Love, if we collar Rashid–"

"Then we have a political nightmare on our hands." Kenton glared at his friend. "Like I said, this is in-country. Without probable cause, we can't go near him."

Marcus scoffed. "Are you telling me he's not still wanted by your FBI?"

Kenton sighed.

"That his whereabouts are not wanted in connection with some kind of tech scandal? Because I find that hard to believe."

"I had Bruno put it in their ear that he is in the country, see if we can get some pressure on him from that direction. But for me to bring them in prematurely, with only a still shot of him standing idle in the lobby, isn't going to do us any good. If it all goes wrong, they have a scapegoat—us."

Olivia sat on the edge of the desk, facing her uncle. Kenton studied her long neck and profile.

"Let's just do what we can from here, protect the Reliance Institute as best as we can, and see if that's enough to find a link. You won't be well received if you have to go to the FBI or any federal institute. You know that," Olivia said.

"Why not?" Kenton frowned as Marcus waved him off.

"Nothing, complete misunderstanding."

He scoffed. That was unlikely. Marcus didn't have misunderstandings. His intentions were usually transparent.

"Marcus, please. Just wait on all this. I know you want Rashid and think with him gone, we'll be safe. But I'm not going to do well if you go off on your own to track him down." Olivia gripped her uncle's hand.

"Of course, dear. I wouldn't even think of going after him alone."

Kenton shook his head as Marcus stood and pulled Olivia into a hug.

"Now, enough of all of this. Kenton, what say you?"

"I told you earlier, I'm here. We do what we can to protect the Institute, and if we have cause to go elsewhere, I'll have your back."

Marcus nodded.

Olivia looked between them and, in silence, left the room.

Kenton frowned and turned to a lying Marcus. "She's not going to back down. She told me earlier that she's worried about you."

Marcus came around the desk, his hands in his pockets. "Ollie has already made it very clear and is using guilt as a way to be merciless against me."

He chuckled as Marcus shook his head.

"She did, however, stick her neck out for you." Marcus turned with a smirk.

"What does that mean?"

"The board felt your line of questioning wasn't direct enough, among other things. You seem to have a reputation, and they felt you have not lived up to it well. The fact you can't guarantee you and your associate cannot keep our technology safe, the attack on Coleston without any solid proof, they're more than a little frustrated. Olivia found their comments ...

outrageous." Marcus grinned. "You would have been impressed with how she brought them down a notch."

Feeling the heat on his face, Kenton clenched his jaw to keep it from falling open.

"You seem to think you're unworthy of what's falling into place. But I'm here to tell you, she finds you very much worthy."

He shook his head, working to find something to say.

"I'm going to look into the email I received."

"Marcus, you promised."

He shrugged. "I never actually promised. Besides, I'm not looking for a fight, not here. I'll wait until he moves to a location where the laws are less favorable."

Kenton sighed. "Let me go with you. Bruno is here, and between him and Drone, your tech is as safe as it can be."

Marcus frowned. "You want to leave again?"

"Marcus."

"She was quite upset last night. At first, I assumed it was the detail I hired. I advised her that she wouldn't be going anywhere without an escort, which made her more than angered. But I think it had more to do with you than the protection."

"I already apologized. I should've said something before I left, but I thought it easier——-"

"Easier? For you?"

He groaned.

"Look." Marcus stepped in front of him, holding his hand out. "This entire thing seems to be moving quickly and, before, I figured she would end up walking. She already told me she was leaving on Thursday. But after her performance with the board, I think she's more taken with you than I realized.

"I know I've pushed more than necessary, but it has been for her protection. But if she's being this protective of you, she's looking at more. Now, is that something you're willing to do? I don't want her hurt."

Feeling even more heat flooding his face and neck, Kenton stepped back. "I've said from the beginning she's too good for me. As much as I would like to be more for her, I'm not certain I can." He tried to swallow, but his mouth was dry. "Look, we've not ... it's not like we've had a discussion. This isn't the focus right now. I'm here. I'll be here until you're both safe. After that, we'll see what happens."

Marcus frowned but nodded. "Then let's go see if my intel is correct."

33

Olivia paced her office, feeling the tension moving up her neck. Rubbing the pained muscle, she collapsed on the small loveseat against the wall and kicked off her shoes. Pulling up her feet, she rotated her neck.

Between the attacks, her injuries, and the stress of the possible hack, her body was feeling the hits. Leaning back, she blew out a heavy breath and closed her eyes.

How could the board think any of this was Kenton's fault? He had worked hard, and between him and Bruno, they had found the information they needed to go after Coleston. If anything, it was more the board's fault for not following through.

A knock made her straighten. Sighing, she stood and walked to the door, opening it to find Kenton.

"What? I know you don't need me to open the door for you."

"I know you're irritated with the board, but that has nothing to do with me. You don't have to take it out on me."

"Trust me, I'm not."

He chuckled and stepped inside, closing the door behind him. His grin widened as he looked her over.

"Did I interrupt your nap?"

She sighed and crossed her arms. "What is it you want?"

He stepped close, making her tense up at his sudden intrusion into her space. It was the first time he had moved in so quickly. Usually, he took his time.

"I'm going with Marcus—"

"What?" Her jaw clenched as he took hold of her waist, holding on despite her stiffness.

"If I go, he'll be careful. He'll have backup if something happens."

"That's not the point. You know you don't have probable cause, and you could lose your badge. Or worse, the both of you end up in jail."

He sighed, wrapping her in a hug. Her confusion continued as she rested her hands at his sides, frowning at the bandage covering his injury.

"I wanted to thank you. Marcus told me you stood up for me with the board. I appreciate that."

"You're not the problem here. They are, and they needed to be told that. I should've known Marcus wouldn't keep things to himself."

He chuckled and kissed the top of her head. "I need to go before Marcus takes off without me."

The stalemate continued, her hands unwilling to release him as his arms kept hold.

She cleared her throat. "Just be careful. With all the attacks, I don't like the thought of both of you in danger."

He sighed and leaned back, those cobalt blues staring. "We'll be safe. Are you staying here?"

She nodded. "I couldn't leave if I wanted to. Marcus has left strict instructions that prevent me from going anywhere alone. I'm not sure I can even go to the lobby."

His eyes searched hers as his fingers played with her hair, tucking it behind her ear and running his thumb down her jaw. "Olivia, I would like to speak with you when this is all over," he whispered.

"About what?" Her heart pounded as she pushed out the words, unsure she should ask.

"Let's just wait. I think ... I think we should wait."

Taking a deep breath, she pushed up on her toes, pulling his cheek down next to hers. "Just be careful, please," she whispered, kissing him.

"No worries." He kissed her cheek and released her quickly, rushing through the door without looking back.

Collapsing back on the loveseat, she worked to calm the pounding of her heart.

"Lord, protect them from themselves, please. I can't lose anyone else."

Her heart constricted. This entire thing with Rashid was taking away the only family she had left. Not to mention Kenton, someone she felt more and more connected to as time passed.

Holding her head in her hands, she worked to ease the emotions of the past few days. She needed a break. She needed help.

"God, please, please protect them both. And please give me strength to get through whatever is coming."

34

"You really think he's here?" Kenton frowned as he studied Marcus.

"My contacts are usually correct."

Kenton scoured the location, noting the entrances and exits as they sat in the parking lot. The busy business center seemed an unlikely place for someone with such an outlandish reputation.

"He was spotted here last week."

"So he might be here for other reasons."

Marcus nodded. "True. And if that's the case, we'll follow him." He leaned back in the seat from behind the steering wheel, narrowing his gaze. "What did Ollie have to say?"

Kenton frowned. "I just wanted to thank her for standing up for me. And ensure she stays in the building."

Marcus chuckled. "I'm sure she appreciated that."

He shrugged. "She didn't get upset. It was a first."

"Hmm ..."

Turning, Kenton grimaced at Marcus's smirk.

"I guess she's getting accustomed to you."

"Look, I know you have ideas—"

"Easy, Kenton. I'm not looking at pushing anything further. I imagine I'll hear enough about it when this is over. She's been dealing, I think."

"Dealing?"

Marcus shrugged. "She's not an outgoing character. She's used to sitting outside the circle and watching those inside."

He chuckled. "I think we have even more in common."

Silence stretched as they watched the building.

His ringtone broke the silence.

"Yeah?"

"Hey, just wondered if we're still on?" Bruno sounded irritated.

"What's wrong?"

"You mean besides the fact we have nothing to stop this attack from happening?"

Kenton sighed. "Look, we're still on call until after midnight. I expect you to keep an eye on things there."

"And you'll be ...?"

"With Marcus. I'll let you know if something pops."

"Yeah, fine."

The call ended, and he dropped the phone in the cupholder.

"Your partner is very good at his job."

Kenton chuckled. "Yes, he is. He's a boy scout and excellent at what he's paid to do."

Marcus chuckled too. "I imagine he won't enjoy what might happen if this hunting expedition goes right."

"Nope, we won't be calling him in," he muttered.

"Perhaps it's time for a walk."

Kenton pushed out of the car, working to catch up to his friend. "You realize if he sees us here, he'll know exactly what we're doing. He could call the police and have us detained."

"Not an issue for me." Marcus's jaw clenched tighter as they strode into the building.

They split up. Kenton took the left as Marcus moved through the right side. Blending in wasn't a problem. Everyone here was dressed in suits and ties, rushing from one place to another.

Pausing at an alcove, he leaned back and searched. Marcus was just ahead of him on the other side, looking at a directory on a large, lit-up board.

As his eyes shifted to the upper deck, thoughts of Olivia drifted into his mind. That fear mounted.

"Let's go."

Coming from his daze, Marcus rushed past, and Kenton followed.

Waiting to speak until they were in the car, he buckled and turned. "What's going on?

"I recognized one of the names on the directory. Seems our old friend has the same habits he did all those years ago."

"Meaning?"

"Did you not do any recon on him before you went in to kill him?"

Kenton glared back. "I went where I was ordered to go. The only recon work I did was scouting the location and finding a better way in, out, and place to set up than you did."

That got him a nasty look.

"Rashid has an import/export business. He's an unnamed partner. That's why I was there in the first place. He traffics women. While I was in the SAS, he became our prime target when we discovered his ties to Britain and the network he had set up there. Let's head back to the office."

"So the SAS just gave up on taking him out?"

Marcus shook his head. "We were ordered to stand down after I returned. Once I had healed, I came back ready to go back in, knowing the lay of the land and the best way to take him out. We were told another interest had picked up that ball, and we were to stand down. It was not a good day for me."

"What's the name of the company?"

"Missions Unlimited. It won't get you anywhere. He and the other partners are too good to slip up."

He texted the name to Bruno. "Still, if we can connect that name to anything else we've found, it'll give us Rashid."

As they pulled into the parking structure, another conversation moved through his mind.

"What did you mean by a misunderstanding?"

Marcus turned. "What?"

"Olivia mentioned you couldn't go to the FBI or any other institution. You called it a misunderstanding."

"It was ..." He mumbled something under his breath.

"What was?"

Marcus sighed. "I had some information that shifted hands after my work for queen and country. I tried to get it to someone who needed to hear it, but no one was willing to listen. It was a ticking time bomb." He sighed heavily.

"I did what I swore never to do and buried it. If it came out, it would be devastating, and I knew it. But no one wanted to listen, and I wouldn't allow myself to be the one to bring it to light. I didn't gather the original intel, so it wasn't my place.

"However, the person that gave it to me was quite adamant it be made known. It needed to be exposed and taken seriously. But it was a black eye."

Kenton's jaw clenched. "What was it?"

"I'm not going to mention it now. It's not important." Marcus's jaw tensed. "When it did come to light, everyone assumed I leaked it, that I had purposely made it known. But it wasn't me. Several federal institutions here tried to pin it on me, blamed me for the leak. Of course it didn't work, but they tried. So your FBI isn't too friendly when it comes to my name."

As they parked, Marcus slid from the seat and Kenton followed. There was no reason to ask. If Marcus Moore had information he didn't want to give up, there was no way it could be pulled from him. He had witnessed that firsthand.

BY THE AFTERNOON, Kenton had set up in the room with the others, going over the security systems in place. Pacing the room while Bruno and Drone worked was more than frustrating. It was boring. This wasn't his wheelhouse.

"I'm going to walk around. I'll be back at six to give you a break."

"Yeah, sounds good," Bruno said without glancing up from the computer.

Stepping from the room, he made his way to Olivia's office. As much as he wanted to speak to her, he was tempting fate. Being around her, holding her, pushed his ability to restrain himself to the brink. Wrapping her up and kissing her breathless was all he could think about, and that would only get him in trouble.

Knocking on the door, he couldn't help but smile. The thought of kissing her made his heart pound.

"Have you heard anything?" Olivia's green eyes lit with hope.

"No, nothing yet. I'm going to take a breather. Bruno and Drone are keeping up with the system." Leaning against the doorframe, he shoved his hands in his pockets to keep himself in check.

"Where's Marcus?"

"In his office. He's been going through some intel, hoping to find some dirt to convince the feds to go after Rashid."

She groaned and turned, making him catch the door before it closed.

Barefoot and pacing, he smiled as he watched her move. She could've been anything—a model, a dancer, even a soccer mom by now. But she'd chosen a singular life, something he found all too relatable.

"When he first told me about the connection, I thought we could find and reinforce the possible weaknesses. Be ready. But after the attacks, the constant emails prodding him, Marcus is losing it." She paused and looked at him, her arms planted firmly on her hips. "He's obsessed."

Stepping in front of her, he shrugged. "There's more at play here than a cyberattack. I know you see that. Rashid is good at making things personal. It's how he works. I'm afraid that no matter what happens tonight, Marcus won't give up his search."

She nodded, biting her bottom lip, drawing his eyes down to watch. Man, he needed to back up.

"I'm headed out for a break. The tech stuff isn't my thing. I'll be back in an hour and here for the rest of the night. Call me if you need something."

Olivia crossed her arms. "I think I can handle sitting here, confined to my office, without any help."

He chuckled, taking hold of her elbow. "That doesn't mean you won't need anything." He winked as she smirked at him.

"And what do you think I need?" She took hold of his arm.

Oh, man.

"You're very good at pushing things. That's what I want to discuss with you another time," he managed to mutter as heat moved across his face.

"Why wait?"

He sighed. Looking into her pretty eyes, he could feel those same demons rising again. Could he ever be good enough for a woman like her?

"I'll see you in an hour." He kissed her forehead before rushing out of the room.

35

After calming his nerves with a short jog, Kenton stepped from the shower, rushing to grab his ringing phone.

"Matthews."

"I've been going over that company you sent me." Bruno's voice kicked up a notch.

A good sign.

"Yeah? What'd you find?"

"Nothing specific, but as I started breaking down the companies involved, another name popped up."

"MetMed Pack?"

"You got it."

He sighed. "It's a connection to Rashid, but not one with his name on it."

"If I had a little more information, we might be able to get names, take them down for the bombing."

He ran his fingers through his wet hair. "That might be a fight for another day. Keep your eyes on the security there. Make sure it's as tight as possible. I'll be back in twenty."

"Got it."

It was a solid enough connection to the bombing, but

without an actual person attached to the company, and Rashid being a silent partner, it would do them no good.

They could send the info to Detective Anders. The only hope to stop the corporation was to build a federal case weighty enough to convince the company to reveal its partners.

With three SWAT members in the hospital after the bombing, it might be enough.

After drying and dressing, he took his time in the kitchen, grabbing a sandwich before returning to the Institute. A knock on his door made him pause.

Peeking through the opening, his heart tightened as he swung it open. "Olivia."

"We need to talk." She pushed past him.

"Okay, but first, where's your protection detail?" He shut the door and turned to see her pacing, her arms crossed and her face splotched red.

"I don't need them. Marcus ... he's... He's gone."

His heart dropped as his appetite left. "Define gone."

"I called him earlier. He said he received an email, and Rashid was threatening him again. He blew it off, said it was just noise to take his attention off the Institute. But now, I can't get ahold of him, and he's not at either house or the apartment."

His jaw twitched. "You've been out running around without any kind of protection?"

"Focus, Kenton."

"Fine. What kind of threat?"

She licked her lips and wiped her face. "He said the email mentioned either him or the girl. I'm guessing he meant me. Marcus said he took care of it, but now—"

"Has Rashid contacted you?"

She shook her head. "I tried to get some help, but I ... I can't find anyone else who would be able to help him."

Standing in the hallway, anger and worry worked their way

through. Once again, if he had only taken out Rashid when he had the chance.

Her phone dinged, and she pulled it from her pocket.

"It's an email." She focused on her phone for a moment before holding it out.

He snatched it away and read the email.

I have Marcus Moore. You have my location. You have three hours to transfer the code, or he dies, slowly.

He handed back the phone and turned. Rage burned through his body as he marched to the kitchen, smashing the dish in the sink and gripping the edge.

"What do we do?"

"*We?*" He spun. "What do *we* do? He's former SAS. You're telling me his country won't take care of this?"

She shook her head. "Any information he might've had is old enough it's not of any use. They won't risk it."

"But they would want Rashid. Call them."

"They won't listen."

He stormed into her space. "How do you know, Olivia? How? Because I can't do this. I'm one man who's out of his prime. My body won't do what it once did, and there's no way I go in there and come out alive against his army. We'll both die."

He tried to hold back, but the situation made him furious. Stepping back, he paced a moment. He never should've let that man live.

"What about our people here?"

She shook her head. "They won't help."

"Why not? They want Rashid, too, I'm certain. If they had the information—"

"No. They won't help." Her voice rose as she glared.

"Why not?" He growled. "Olivia, I won't help unless I know the whole thing. What are you not telling me?"

Her jaw jumped as she wiped her face. "When he couldn't get back into the SAS, he looked for other ways to use his skills."

"No way. He wouldn't flip."

She shook her head. "No, he most definitely did not. But he picked and chose what jobs to take and why. Standing up to rebel commanders who took out villages, wiped people out. Stopping shipments of guns from getting into the wrong hands. But then, he came across a ... a delicate situation." She swallowed hard.

"The misunderstanding," he mumbled.

She nodded. "There was a unit in Haiti. They were supposed to help the villages with supplies and then weed out the rebels. If the village had good information, they were given the supplies and left alone. If they didn't, the commander ..." she shook her head. "They moved in and spread across the country, taking out villages that don't help --—"

"Wait, you're telling me that Marcus released the information about the Mushroom Effect?"

"He didn't. He tried to bury it, but the man who had given him the intel let it out."

He let out a guttural groan as he began to pace.

"What they were doing was evil! They killed hundreds of people just because they refused to give up information or it was bad information." Her voice rose.

"Of course it was evil." His body ached at the memory. "It was horrible, and the men responsible should've been tried and thrown in jail or stood in front of a firing squad."

"He gave them a chance." She pushed into his space. "He sent the president copies of the pictures, the video. He shared with anyone who would listen. But when they didn't act, he tried to bury it. He knew the consequences."

"Then why didn't he stop the person who actually leaked it?" He moved in, backing her against the wall. "What was released painted the entire country, my country, as evil. The entire world thought of us as hate-filled, bloodthirsty men who took and killed whoever they pleased!

"It destroyed peace talks and wreaked havoc on the men and women trying to keep peace in other areas of the world. They were attacked, killed because of what was revealed. Besides, how did he even know the president received the information? How did he even know it was pushed as high as it needed to go?"

He slammed his fist into the wall behind her. "What did he think would happen once he released evidence that our country was the most hated and feared in the world? It destroyed and killed more men and women than possible because he didn't take care of it right then." He straightened, his throat burning.

"I lost friends because of that. Good people. People who didn't deserve that kind of disrespect. It might've only been a single unit that was at fault, but the second the information hit the world stage, it may as well have been anyone in uniform. It was worse than Vietnam. Worse than any catastrophe that had hit us," he whispered.

Backing away, he took a breath and headed to his room. Yanking out his duffle bag, he threw it on the bed and started packing all his gear.

"He didn't leak it, Kenton. He tried to bury it when they didn't listen. He knew how devastating it would be."

Ignoring her, he loaded his ammunition kits.

"What ... what're you doing?" her shaky voice sounded behind him.

"I'm packing."

"You said you wouldn't come out alive."

He shook his head. "I won't. But this is my fault. I should've killed Rashid when I had the chance."

"What happened?"

"Olivia."

"Ollie."

"I like Olivia." He turned with a glare as her face reddened. "And I don't talk about it."

Going to his closet, he pulled down more equipment and his lockbox.

"I guess this is why I never had friends, relationships. God knew this would be how I would die," he muttered under his breath as he shoved the gear into the bag.

Yanking out his rifle case, he went to the gun safe and opened it. "Not nearly enough," he mumbled.

"What're you saying?"

"Just reminding myself how bad an idea this is."

Shoving his gear in the bag, he secured his rifle, then put the rest of the weapons in a hardback case. Pulling it onto his shoulder, he grabbed his rifle case and duffle.

He brushed past her to the hallway. "I need all the correspondence between Marcus and Rashid, including all of Marcus's files on him. He already told me he thought he knew where Rashid might be located."

She pushed in front of him before he reached the door. "I'm going with you."

"Uh, no." He started past and she stopped him, planting a hand on his chest.

"You're being crazy! You can't go after him alone!"

"You're right. I am crazy. This whole thing is crazy, and there's no possible way I'm getting out alive." He dropped his duffle and set down the rifle case. "In fact ..." He gripped the sides of her face and pulled her in, kissing her hard.

Her hands went from pushing to pulling him in, gripping his shirt as she rose to meet him. After an earthshaking moment, she lowered.

Resting his forehead against hers, his thumbs moved along her jaw, his heart pounding in his ears.

"See? Crazy," he muttered.

As he moved his thumb across her bottom lip, he was about to kiss her again when she stepped back.

"I'm going, or you don't get the information you need." Her soft voice echoed in the quiet hallway as she swiftly exited through the door.

He let out a breath, watching her leave. "That went … well."

Working to ease his breathing and his heart rate, he grabbed up the duffle bag and rifle case. No sense getting attached now. He was done for after this.

He groaned, following her out the door and to the waiting car.

36

———

Sitting in the car, Olivia gripped the wheel, trying to ease her emotions. Her training was one thing, but she had never had to deal with a man like Kenton Matthews before. If she had stayed with the SAS, she would be more seasoned, but right now, she felt like she had just given part of herself up to a man who seemed rather convinced he was about to die.

Get a grip.

Bags hit the back seat before the door slammed shut, then the passenger door opened. Kenton slid inside, slamming the door as she took off.

"Details, now."

She shook her head. "I'm going with you."

"You know what he's doing to Marcus, right? You said you've seen his chest. That's what he does, and he enjoys it. There's no way I'm letting you anywhere near him."

She gritted her teeth.

"That's why we don't do family and close friends. Anyone we contact could become a target, even after all these years. I don't mind my military friends. They can take care of themselves, but anyone else ..."

"What about your partner?"

"What about him?"

"He's excellent with computers."

"Nope, out of the question. There's no way I'm bringing Bruno along. He can't handle it. He doesn't know when to step back and wait. He's not trained."

"He's your weakness." She could feel his eyes on her as she drove, weaving through traffic and heading to the Institute.

"Bruno?"

She glanced to see Kenton on the phone. His strong jaw had a day's worth of stubble that made his lips seem that much brighter. She shook her head.

"Good grief," she mumbled.

This was crazy. Marcus was in danger, and all she could think about was that kiss.

"I'm on my way. Don't leave the station, Bruno. You understand me?" He shoved the phone into the cup holder.

"What's wrong? Why is he at the station?" She shifted lanes and turned right toward the police station.

"Bruno left a little after me to take a break. He thinks he's being followed. He was at the station running tags of a car following him. They came back stolen."

"That means he knows about your life too," she whispered.

He nodded. "Told you ... keeping contact, getting close. Even though we thought we got out, it was never certain."

She chewed on her bottom lip, hating the fact he was right. "It's my fault."

"What? How does this have anything to do with you?"

"Marcus blocked my advance in the program."

"I can understand that."

She snapped her head to glare at him. "What?"

"I would never want someone in my family involved in that kind of career, especially a woman."

"Isn't that my decision?" Her face heated as she turned back to the traffic.

"It is." His soft voice made her shake her head.

"When he blocked me from moving on, I joined the military. I enjoyed it, but it wasn't what I wanted. I made him feel guilty all the time, complained he had taken away my one chance. That's why he asked me to come here." She swallowed.

Kenton gripped her arm, pulling her hand away from the wheel and intertwining her fingers. "He's strong, and I know he would never blame you. This isn't on you. It's all Rashid. He would've taken Marcus whether you were here or not."

She chewed on her bottom lip as Kenton's lips brushed her hand. Her eyes went wide as she tried to focus on the road.

The rest of the drive was silent until she pulled up in front of the station. She came around the front of the car and found Kenton's hand in hers.

"I can wait here."

"No, you're not to leave my sight. Not yet." He pulled her along behind him.

They rushed up the stairs and through the metal detectors. She released two guns and a knife before they let her through to the elevators.

"Bruno?" He pulled her to a desk and peered down at her. "Wait here."

She yanked her hand free and crossed her arms with a glare.

"Olivia, wait, please." He ground the words out, but she appreciated the effort.

Leaning against the desk, she pulled out her phone as Kenton walked past her to Bruno. She watched the hushed conversation before Bruno's voice rose.

"What? He's what?"

She rolled her eyes. Kenton was right. Bruno wasn't someone they could involve.

"Easy, man. We need to talk." Kenton motioned her over, and she followed them into a small room.

"Ollie."

"Thanks, but I'd rather stay focused here." She held up her hand at Bruno's advance and he nodded.

"Olivia, the location?"

She sighed. Pulling up the emails, she sent the paper trail to Kenton's phone, including the file Marcus had already shown her that gave all the information he would need on Rashid.

"Okay, we need some eyes. I need the plans so I can see where we're going."

"I have those for when we get there."

He glared. "You're not going."

She pushed into his space. "I already know where it is. I know the layout better than you. I can easily get us in and out."

"You can't go. If Rashid gets to you …" His jaw clenched.

She narrowed her eyes as he struggled to finish that sentence. "I can take care of myself. Marcus knows that."

"Not against Rashid." Kenton's voice rose. "You don't know him."

"I've read all the material, and I know how he works. I've done the research and have his profile memorized."

"You haven't had to see him work!"

Fear flashed in his eyes, his face paling as he walked to the back of the room. He paced a moment, rubbing his forehead. "You don't understand. He doesn't kill, he tortures. You will endure and he'll keep going. I won't let you near him."

She bit her lip, feeling more enamored and angered. He wanted to protect her, keep her safe, but it really wasn't his call.

"I'll stay in the van. We'll need tech support."

He paused, gripping his hips as his blue eyes burned into hers. "Promise."

She shook her head. "No, I won't. But that's as good as you're going to get."

He licked his lips and nodded. "Send the info to Bruno." He turned to his partner. "You see what you can do from here. Keep in contact with Olivia, and between both of you, maybe you can give me something."

"Wait, you're going in? Alone?"

Kenton glared. "We don't have much choice."

"Call in the SWAT team, the cops, the Marines. This isn't a simple kidnapping. This is a psychopath within the United States. I say we go in full tilt and take him out."

"I know what he is, Bruno. By the time we arrive, I doubt Rashid will still be there. He'll leave it up to his paid personnel, and no one will know who they work for, and there will be no trace of him. Besides, we have nothing implicating him as the kidnapper. You know that email won't be traced."

Bruno's face went red as he stared at Kenton. "It's not your job."

"It was a long time ago. Now I'll finish it. Even if I don't get out, if he's there, he'll die too." Kenton turned and left the room.

"You can't let him do this."

She frowned at Bruno. "Who do you think told him? I don't have anyone else who can help me. The email is untraceable, so it's not probable cause. There is no other legal way inside. I can only do so much, and I trust Kenton."

"So, you don't care if he dies as long as he tries, huh?"

She leaned into Bruno's space, her heart pounding as she glared. "Don't confuse needing his help with indifference to his safety. I care about him dearly but Marcus is the only family I have. What would you do?"

Bruno only frowned.

"Keep the line open and stay here until it's over. I wouldn't leave alone if I were you." She turned and strode out the door to Kenton as he got off the desk phone.

"Let's go." He headed toward the elevators.

37

K enton reached back, pleased when Olivia put her hand in his without his asking.

"We have to make a stop first."

"What?" He paused.

"I need more equipment."

He frowned as she pulled away, going to the driver's side of the car. Sliding into the seat, Bruno's words rattled in his head. It was his job, one he should've finished long ago.

The car started to move and with a grunt, he pushed his seat all the way back, pulling the case from the back seat to the floorboard. He couldn't just sit here doing nothing. Taking out each gun, he checked the slides and loaded the chambers, filling the extra clips with bullets.

"Why didn't you kill him?"

He swallowed and shook his head. "It was his son's birthday party. The only clear shot I had, he was holding his baby daughter in his hands. I ... I couldn't do it."

Olivia gripped his arm. "Marcus was right."

His head snapped to her.

"He said you always did the right thing, no matter the cost.

He told me he begged you to leave him, walk away so you could escape, but you refused. Now, to hear that ..." She nodded. "You did the right thing."

"No, I gave up my objective and hundreds of people have died because of me. That's when I got out. If I couldn't keep my emotions out of it, then it was time for me to move on."

"You did the right thing."

He shook his head. A tug on his arm made him turn. Her hair fell around her face from her messy bun and his heart pounded. What she had been through and the fighter she had become ... she was amazing. Even with her only family being held hostage, she didn't blame him.

"You know, if this hadn't happened, I planned to ask you out." He grinned as she dropped his hand, red rushing to her cheeks.

"Not the time," she whispered.

He chuckled and continued checking his weapons. "Actually, this might be the only time."

Setting down the gun, he watched her shoulders stiffen, her eyes scanning the road ahead of them.

"Kenton."

"Olivia." He leaned on the console, wondering just how he was going to manage another kiss.

She turned into a storage facility, and he sat back in the seat, avoiding the cameras. Old habits died hard. He frowned as they pulled through and parked outside a large unit.

"What's in here?" He got out and watched as she approached the unit, putting in her code and unlocking the latch.

"It belongs to Marcus and to me. We keep what we need away from the houses and in here."

He helped pull up the door, then wrapped an arm around her waist as they walked in.

"You know, even as a teenager, I thought a woman with a British accent was the sexiest thing." He squeezed her waist.

She huffed, the start of a smirk on her lips. "Close the door."

With a chuckle, he let go and pulled the door back down. A dim light barely illuminated the area as he stood to the side. She tried to reach around him, allowing him to pull her in again. She flipped a switch, and a generator kicked on. Flashing lights fluttered and then beamed brightly as the hum of booting computers echoed in the room.

"Equipment, huh?" He looked down at her still in his grip.

Studying her face, he found himself again drawn to her lips as her eyes searched his.

"I ... I need to get things together," she whispered.

He sighed and released her. Maybe it just wasn't meant to be.

"If we do get some help, they'll be here soon."

"Help?" He crossed his arms as she pulled a few rifle cases and other equipment from a shelf. "What help?"

She heaved a sigh. "I ... I don't know. I tried to call, but they didn't answer."

He leaned against a workbench, staring. She seemed oblivious, gathering gear and strapping on her tactical vest before loading it down. If they had help ... but what kind of help?

Motion in a monitor grabbed his attention. A van had pulled up outside the unit.

"Friends?"

She nodded and opened the door remotely.

"Ollie?" A tall man with a British-laced accent walked in, fully decked out in his gear. The man raised a gun at him instantly as a dark-haired man followed. "Who's he?"

"He's a friend. Why didn't you answer me?"

"You really thought we wouldn't come?" Another man stepped forward, shorter than the other two.

"You didn't answer," she muttered, obviously upset.

"Who's the American?"

He studied the three men. They were all older than him, closer to Marcus's age.

"Marcus must've forgotten to mention me." He grinned at their confusion.

Olivia joined the three. "He's Kenton Matthews."

This was met with startled stares, and he shook his head, straightening from the bench. He took hold of Olivia's arm before she moved away. "Why didn't you tell me you called others in?"

"They didn't answer me. They always answer."

He moved closer. "But you didn't think I needed to know? I was expecting to die in there, and you could've at least told me there was a chance."

"I didn't know there was a chance. Why would I mention it? If they don't return the message, that means they're out." Her voice rose.

"Excuse me. I'm assuming we're on a time frame here, correct?" one of the men asked.

Kenton nodded curtly and made his way past the men to the car. Grabbing his gear from the back seat, he brought it inside and loaded up. "A little heads up's all I was asking for. I already called and had my will mailed to Bruno."

"That doesn't mean it won't happen. You're pretty young to think you'll make it out alive."

He frowned at their chuckles, strapping his rifle at his side. "Let's just say I was misled into thinking I was going in alone."

She glared back at him as they finished loading the equipment. As he walked past, she gripped his arm and turned him to face her. "Are you mad because you have help or because I asked someone else?"

His arm tensed under her fingers.

"If you think I was willing to run to you first, to send you in there alone, you really are crazy. I did everything I could before coming to you because I knew no matter how bad it looked, you would run in and die for him." A sheen covered her eyes as she walked away, and his heart fluttered again.

She was trying to protect him. He had never had anyone other than teammates want to save him, and this woman had tried her best.

Man, he loved her.

"Come on, lover-boy. We've got to get going." The British accent made him smirk as he got into the van, finding a seat as Olivia handed him a large tablet.

"Drive, Sebastian. We have to discuss the operation." Her accent thickened, and he smiled.

Maybe this wasn't the end after all.

38

After going through the blueprints and assuming the correct locations of all the exits, they had a rather flimsy plan in place. But at least he had backup.

Parked half a mile from Rashid's warehouse, Kenton sized up the men sitting in the van with him. Sebastian was obviously in charge. Then there was Gus, the short, bespectacled man, and the third, Charles.

"Bruno wants to know the plan."

He frowned at Olivia. "He can't know. If he can manage a satellite signal to see movement inside or get us info about whether or not Rashid is for sure in there, that will help."

"Halil Rashid?"

He nodded at the scowl on Charles's face, and the mood in the van turned even more somber as muttered curses rumbled between the men.

"Let's go."

They piled out of the van as Olivia stepped out.

"No, love. Marcus would never approve." Sebastian took her arm.

"I'm going in."

"No, you're not." He glared as she lifted her chin and returned his stare.

"We need eyes and backup. I'll stay with her and head your way whenever you start to exit. I'll keep you covered."

He nodded to Gus, who pulled at Olivia's hand before getting back in the van.

Her face red, she looked determined to speak. He went nose-to-nose with her, ready to argue. She took hold of his vest.

"You're staying here." He gazed into her green eyes.

"I ... I was going to offer a good luck kiss."

Taking hold of her waist with his free hand, he lowered his head partway, letting her grip his neck and close the distance. A feathery kiss landed on his lips, then she pulled back.

"You'll get the rest of that when you get Marcus back," she whispered.

"Is this another play?"

She shook her head as tears ran down her face. "I don't play with hearts."

Wiping her cheek, he kissed her forehead and turned to catch up to the men, working to find his focus.

As he fell in behind them, he cleared his throat. "You two go for Marcus. I'm looking for Rashid."

"Wandering around that place won't help you out. Breaking her heart won't either," Sebastian said.

"As long as Rashid is alive, she and Marcus will always be in danger. That ends tonight."

The two men nodded as they approached the compound.

***

WEAVING THROUGH TREES AND BRUSH, Kenton found himself back in his element even after all the years out. His training took over, and his body breezed silently across the terrain until they reached the fence that surrounded the compound.

Rashid's house was more of an old warehouse. The blueprints showed the changes he had made inside, including split-level living quarters and several rooms on the ground level. Marcus would be in one of them.

Sebastian took his time with the lock on the gate, then opened it slowly. No alarm. He wasn't sure if Olivia or Bruno had helped with that, but he was grateful.

A red Range Rover sat in the compound lot, and he motioned to the men. Rashid was always ostentatious, and that bright red vehicle with chrome all around spoke volumes. He was still here.

Advancing behind the two probable former SAS members, he allowed them to do the work as he searched for signs of Marcus or Rashid.

"Go right." Olivia's voice in his ear took his focus for a moment as he followed.

Several men sat around a table, laughing and eating. Sebastian rolled a gas bomb into the room and sealed the door. Barely a sound was heard as the bomb detonated and silenced the men inside.

Turning a corner, he noticed an alarm on one of the doors, the wire moving across the doorframe and up to the ceiling. He motioned to the men and offered cover as Sebastian got to work on the lock.

"We see it. Give us a moment." Gus's voice and breath remained even.

Charles tapped his shoulder, and he backpedaled until a hand stopped him. Farther down the hall, a man rounded the corner and headed their way.

"Out," he muttered, and Sebastian pulled away from the door to their cover inside the opposite hallway.

The man passed by, oblivious as he spoke on his phone.

"He's expecting company, then he'll call you." The Arabic-speaking man nodded as he turned the corner.

"We've got the alarm, you get the latch." Olivia's voice sounded firm, calm.

Sebastian returned to work until Kenton's impatience got the best of him. Pulling the man back, he jammed a hook into the door and kicked it open.

Marcus hung from the wall, bloodied, beaten, and too still.

"Get him and go. I've got an idea."

The other two nodded as Kenton closed the door and crept down the hallway, finding the warehouse kitchen. In the blueprints, it was a central room, large and perfect for a distraction. Easing inside, it was devoid of men and full of equipment.

Searching the supplies, he pulled out bottles of oil. He kept an eye out for a timer as he saturated the area. Stacking paper towels and napkins from the pantry in the oil slick, he yanked down an old electric heater.

He plugged it in, shoved some of the paper towels in the front, then cranked the knob all the way up and hurried out of the room. Locking the door, he slammed it closed and then jammed the mechanism with a hard blow from the butt of his rifle.

"They can't get out." Gus's voice took his attention as he advanced back to the corridor where he'd left the men.

Gunfire sent tension rippling through him as he turned the corner. Taking aim, he picked off three men from behind and moved swiftly down the corridor.

"They're headed for the exit. On my way."

He followed, taking out a few more men and then covering the others from the inside. Once they moved through to the outside, he closed and locked the door, then went left, looking for Rashid.

"Get out. What are you doing?" Olivia's hiss came through the line, and he took out his earwig.

He rounded a corner, senses alert to sudden movement.

The group of men waiting for him opened fire, and he felt the sting of a shot across his shoulder as he jumped back.

His shots were finding their targets, but he was running low on ammo. He needed to find Rashid before he ran out.

Turning back the way he came, he took out three more men before a powerful jolt knocked him unconscious.

39

Staring at the screen, Olivia watched two men hoist Kenton by his arms and drag him down the hall.

"No," she shouted.

A thump at the door made her leap to open it.

"Why did you leave him? Go back and get him right now!"

She helped heave Marcus into the van, stifling a sob at his pale and bloodied appearance.

"Marcus needs us. Besides, your American has other intentions."

"They've got him. Shocked him and have him ... Oh no," she muttered as the bloody marks across Marcus's body took her breath. "He ... He—"

"Matthews will take care of it."

She looked up at Charles with a glare. "I just told you they have him. Rashid will do this and worse to Kenton."

Grabbing her guns, she pushed past the men and fled into the woods, willing her body to calm. She couldn't lose him. Not now. In all her life, she had never met someone like Kenton, and she accepted what she'd known all along. She had already given her heart to him, long before that first kiss. She wasn't about to lose him.

"The men are leaving the compound. Matthews must've left something for them. They're headed your way. Hunker down, love, until they pass."

She slinked down into the tall grass, surrounding herself in the trees as she followed Sebastian's advice.

"Hang on, Kenton. Please."

SHAKING HIS HEAD, Kenton woke, dizzy and nauseated from the shock. His neck burned as the pressure in his shoulders took center stage.

"You made it." Halil Rashid's sick voice made him sigh. "I didn't want to start without you. Besides, your friend was no fun. He passed out much too soon. His old age, I assume."

"Yeah, well, don't beat yourself up. I'm sure you tried your best." A blow to his stomach took his breath for a moment.

His shoulders burning and hands numb, Kenton realized he had taken Marcus's place. His arms hung above his head, and bearing his weight, he was too weak to pull himself up.

"So, let's begin with Ollie."

He sighed. "Who's Ollie?"

A slice across his chest made him clench his teeth, refusing to offer the man what he wanted.

"It will only get worse, Matthews. You see, I had no idea you were still in the game. But this whole thing with Moore, well, I was all too eager to ruffle his feathers. I don't really need access from you or Moore. I have my own."

A cut across his thigh burned as he held his tongue. At least that confirmed their suspicion that Coleston was the mole. If Rashid got away, Kenton had no doubts Bruno would find him through the mole.

"I'm not in the game," he mumbled.

"Oh, I think you are." Rashid grinned maniacally as the next slice hit across his midsection, burning down to his toes. "I'm starting shallow, just so you know. It allows this process to last so much longer."

A knock on the door dimmed Rashid's smile as he turned.

"What?" he screamed as a man entered.

The faint odor of smoke permeated the room, and Kenton managed a grin.

"Sir, you have to know." The trembling man pointed to the hallway as the smoky haze filtered in from the hall.

Another slice to his side made him tense. Rashid dropped the knife on the table with the others, then stepped into the hallway.

Looking down at his feet, Kenton noticed a small ledge where his shackles attached to their anchor hooks. He managed to twist and rest the sides of his feet on the hooks, allowing the chain holding his shoulders to loosen.

His hands hung lower than his shoulders, and he worked his fingers, knowing he needed them to escape.

Shouting came from the door, and he turned, allowing his body to hang once again.

Rashid lunged into his face. "Where did they take Marcus?"

He smirked and used his remaining strength to push his lower body against the wall and slam his head into Rashid's.

The man screamed and fell backward, rising with blood gushing from his nose. Rashid attacked, using Kenton's torso as a punching bag. He tightened and braced as much as he could until a hit to his diaphragm made his breath hitch. Another hit had him gasping for air as he blacked out, a painless peace washing over.

40

Wading through the brush, Olivia carefully picked her path toward the warehouse. The men had scattered. They were probably more worried about the smoke billowing from the central room than whether someone else was trying to get inside.

Opening the door, she allowed her eyes to adjust to the dim light and the smoke hanging in the air.

"Go left to where you disabled the lock. That's probably where he'll be. Sebastian is on his way."

She nodded at Gus's voice and continued on the route Kenton had taken.

Turning corners carefully, she managed to avoid the men running for the outer doors. Checking each room in the corridor, she came up empty and shook her head.

"Where are you, Kenton? Please hang on."

The fumes built and burned her eyes and lungs as the shrill fire alarm pierced her ears. A few sprinklers had turned on, showering her in certain hallways. Footprints crisscrossed the floor, but there was nothing to indicate where they would've taken Kenton.

Sidestepping bodies, she paused at the sound of boots stomping on the concrete floor. Hiding in an alcove, she waited for the men to pass. The footsteps stopped and her heart pounded harder. If the steps weren't running away from the fire, they were heading in her direction.

Edging around to another hallway, she observed drag marks through the pooling water. As she studied them, a man stumbled onto her position. He fumbled for his weapon.

Before he could fire, she landed a sharp blow to his neck and then swept his feet out from under him.

"Over here!"

Rushing into another corridor, she sank into the shadows as more footsteps neared. Two men walked past. The third paused. He turned.

Taking three shots, three men fell to the ground.

Her earpiece crackled. "You're going in too deep. They're going to find you."

"Then this is where he is," she mumbled.

A scream made her pause.

"Kenton."

OPENING HIS EYES, Kenton took several strained breaths as he balanced on the hooks once again. The room was empty, and the door stood open as smoke poured inside. Straining, he gradually moved his hands closer together, pushing at his thumb until the joint dislocated with a quick release of pain.

He used his weight to shove his hand through the shackle, taking some skin off as the metal scraped and burned. Doing the same to his other hand, he forced his way through. Once free, he popped his thumbs back in, grimacing.

Chains rattled around his ankles as he made his way to the

table, where he broke the locks with a fire rod. Shoving a knife into his waistband, he took two more and headed for the exit.

His boots to the side of the doorway caught his eye, and he smiled at the butt of his knife sticking from the top. Lacing them up, leg sheath back in place, he then eased out the door.

Thick smoke obscured the area. He crouched, moving slowly through the fog. Finding his footing, he stilled as a man came running down the hallway and then lunged, slicing the man's leg and silencing him. He tied the man's shirt around his nose and mouth.

Working through the maze of rooms, he finally got his bearings when he ended up at the room where they had found Marcus.

Turning the corner, he froze. Rashid stood in the hallway, Olivia in his grasp.

41

———————

"I t looks like I win either way." Rashid sneered, his knife resting against Olivia's throat.

"You're dead." Kenton's gaze moved between Olivia and Rashid.

She could take him, but the fear in her eyes—that wasn't the woman he knew.

"You don't understand. She's not what you're expecting."

Rashid chuckled, dropping his grip on her waist and running his fingers down her cheek. That spark returned, fire and anger flashing in her eyes.

"I had no idea this woman was so close to you or Marcus. He's done a good job of hiding her."

Come on, Olivia. Drop him.

"You seem troubled." Rashid's guttural laughter twisted his insides.

"The police are on their way. This fire, this compound. There's no way you escape without leaving traces of your DNA behind." He used the shirt around his mouth and nose to wipe away the blood from headbutting Rashid. "See? I've got proof this was all you. You're not going anywhere."

Rashid smiled that crooked smile he'd seen too many times. "First, I'll kill this beautiful woman as you watch. Then I'll kill you. Marcus, if he survives, will suffer much longer."

"Tell me why." Olivia's whispered voice hung in the air.

"Why? You don't know?" Rashid chuckled. "It's what I do. It's the game we play." He pushed his face into Olivia's cheek. "And I always win."

"You don't even know me," she murmured.

"Who are you? Ollie, I'm assuming." Rashid sighed. "Too bad we don't have more time to make this a much more pleasant ending."

In the blink of an eye, she twisted his wrist, making him drop the knife. She slammed her elbow into his neck, then kicked his legs out from under him. Rashid sat up to attack, but Olivia brought her arm around and positioning him in a headlock from behind, silenced him with one quick move.

Rushing to her side, he pulled her in closer, surveying the area from over her head. She took several breaths before returning his hug, burying her face in his neck.

"Gus says we need to go. The fire trucks have been dispatched. Sebastian has our exit covered," she said as he nodded, gripping her hand and pulling her toward the open door.

Once in the woods, she ran in front of him, jogging to the van. He caught up and playfully pushed her shoulder. "You came to get me."

She groaned. "Not now, Kenton."

He grabbed her hand somewhat gingerly, pulling her around and into him. "About the rest of that kiss."

She backed away, staring at his chest.

"Olivia."

"You're ... you need a hospital."

Lifting her chin, he smiled and leaned in closer. "It's fine.

Doesn't hurt. I just want you to admit you cared enough to come find me."

"This is not the time."

"I'm in love with you, Olivia."

"What?"

Grabbing her waist, he pulled her in and stole a kiss, breathing her in as he slowly eased back.

"You ... you can't say that," she whispered.

"I can. You just don't want to admit you love me too. Not yet, anyway." He smirked as she backed away and put her hands on her hips.

"Don't act like you know me so well."

"Gotta get to the van. The sirens are getting louder." He winked and hustled past, chuckling to hear her coming up behind him.

"You can't assume something like that. That's not how this works. I was worried to death."

"Keep telling yourself that."

She hit his shoulder, and he winced. "Easy. I was just tortured."

"That's not going to be the worst part of your day if you don't take back what you said."

He smiled as Sebastian came into view, motioning them to hurry.

Collapsing on the van floor, he groaned as he rolled onto his back.

"You're not looking so well." Marcus's voice barely sounded as he turned to see his friend, pale and gasping for breath.

"Marcus? Did you clear him?" He looked at Charles.

"I think it's a punctured lung. We can't fix him here."

Olivia shoved at Gus's shoulder. "Get to the hospital, fast."

"We can't explain this."

"I don't care. I didn't almost die saving his butt only for him to die on me now." Kenton rolled Marcus to his side. "Don't you die on me. Not now. Not after all of this," he whispered.

42

Opening his eyes, Kenton inhaled deeply and gazed around the room.

Olivia sat sound asleep in the chair next to his bed. Behind her, Marcus lay in the next bed, tubes and monitors all around him.

Besides the damage done from the knife wounds, Marcus's lung was ruptured. It took several hours for him to come out of surgery. Kenton had waited with Olivia, attempting to keep her calm as she applied gauze to his wounds and paced while mumbling about the stubborn men in her life.

Marcus had survived the surgery but had a long road to recovery. And after waiting so long, Kenton barely remembered getting on the gurney before blacking out.

But Olivia was here, sitting beside him, waiting for him to wake up. He smiled.

The door opened, and Sebastian stood glancing at him as Bruno stopped and raised his palms. Kenton waved him through.

"Oh, man. What did he do?"

Looking down, Kenton frowned at the stitched-up wounds

and purple skin. Pulling the blanket up, he caught Bruno's eye. "What's going on?"

"I can't stop it, man."

Kenton frowned. "Stop what?"

"The fire didn't destroy what I think you were hoping it would destroy. Lots of blood, clothes, people still around."

"It is what it is. I'm just glad to get out alive." Kenton grinned as Bruno shook his head. "Any problems with the system at the Institute?"

"Nothing. Not one attempt."

"We need to push Coleston. He's the mole. Rashid confirmed it."

"Not sure you're in any position to convince the board it was him."

The door opened and another man entered in full uniform, a familiar glare on his face.

"Uh-oh," Bruno woke Olivia and sent her to standing.

"Who are you?" She crossed her arms and intercepted the man as he studied Marcus with a frown.

The man's gaze shifted to Kenton.

"Olivia, this is the chairman of the Joint Chiefs. General Cotton."

She turned with wide eyes as General Cotton made his way to Kenton's bed. "You don't look as bad as I've seen you before," Cotton smirked as he shook his hand.

"I'll heal." Kenton nodded.

Bruno cleared his throat and motioned to Kenton's chest. The General pulled back the blanket.

"I think you should go." He scowled at Bruno, who took off like a shot.

"That's worse."

Kenton frowned, pulling the blanket back up.

Cotton glanced between him and Marcus. "So, it's what it appears?"

"Exactly what it appears, sir."

Cotton nodded. "For the record, I've been briefed by an Agent McMurry."

"Yes, sir?"

"He's put in a request for a company that we've been watching closely. Missions Unlimited. I think we're about to get some answers on their previous dealings as well as a bombing that happened a few days ago. Put several of his men in the hospital. I think we're going to cinch all this up."

That was good news.

General Cotton paused. "For the record, who killed Halil Rashid?"

"I did." Kenton ignored the glare from Olivia, hoping Cotton wouldn't ask any more questions.

General Cotton nodded and left.

He motioned Olivia over and took her elbow, pulling until he got her hand. "Before you get mad, let me explain."

She nodded.

"If they know you did it, there would be an investigation into you and Marcus. You're not an American, number one, and I don't want them to uncover anything else." He pulled her closer. "If I did it, Cotton can say it was sanctioned, and considering the circumstances, it gets tied up in a nice, neat bow."

He sighed as she chewed on her bottom lip. "I know you want to go back. If you need me to, I will officially change the report to state you took care of an international terrorist by yourself."

She slid onto the bed beside him, leaning over his body as her arm held her up. "What makes you think I want to go back?" Her pretty eyes searched his.

"Marcus mentioned it. You also made a comment. I thought maybe you wanted to get back in." His focus went askew as his eyes landed on her lips. His breathing kicked up.

She smiled. "That might've been before I found something to keep me here."

He grinned as she leaned down and finished the kiss she had promised. As she pulled back, he held the back of her neck, keeping her close.

"You might want to close the curtain next time you do that." He grinned as she turned to the other side of the room.

The three former SAS agents were standing, glaring at them. She chuckled and stood, sliding the curtain closed, then moved back into his arms, kissing him several times over.

EPILOGUE

Three Months Later

Standing in the kitchen with Olivia, Kenton smiled at the pie she had made from scratch. From the homemade crust to the filling, she'd insisted on his help.

Aside from being her taste tester, however, she hadn't let him do much else.

As she fitted the crust over the top, the sight of her domestic side struck a nerve, and his admiration skyrocketed.

"Then you cut the slits and brush it with the egg wash. See?" She held up the finished product, and he nodded as she slid it into the oven. "Now, you get to clean up since I did all the work."

He chuckled. "Deal."

She turned and draped her apron on the chairback as he gathered the dishes. With his hands full, she tossed a handful of flour at his face. Her laughter rang through the kitchen as he set his load in the sink and smirked, wiping the white dust off. Taking a handful and turning, she backed out of the room.

"Kenton, I was just playing. I've got enough flour on me."

"I think you need more."

As he chased her down the hallway and around the sectional, her laughter filled the house. He cornered her at the pillar in the dining room. Pulling her around, he grinned as she squeezed her eyes shut. Dumping the flour on the floor, he leaned in and kissed her, pulling her in and taking his time.

Her hands settled around his neck, pulling him down. He leaned away just enough to free his lips.

"Marry me, Olivia." Opening his eyes, he found her staring.

"I—"

"I love you, and I know you love me." He grinned as her cheeks went bright red.

"I do love you."

He kissed her again, finally hearing the words he had been anticipating for the past three months. Three months of something wonderful he had never had in his entire life. Three months of laughter and happiness. It was new, exciting, and made his heart pound.

She stepped back, leaning against the pillar and looking up at him. "Marriage is a commitment, something I'm not sure we're ready for. I mean, it's only been three months."

He nodded with a sigh. "It is, and it has been. But I've waited a long time for you. I didn't even realize I was waiting. I just figured marriage wasn't for me. I'm not taking this lightly."

She bit her bottom lip, those wheels turning in her mind. Stepping back to the couch, he sat on the back, pulling her between his knees.

"What's on your mind?"

"We've not really talked about what we want."

"I want you. What do you want?"

Taking a few steps back, she crossed her arms and chewed on her bottom lip again. His nerves took a hit.

What could she possibly want that made her so reluctant to agree?

"I just … I've always seen myself getting married someday and having a family. I didn't have that, and for some reason, if I can, I would like a family." Her green eyes met his and he smiled, reaching out and pulling her back in.

"That's what this is about?"

"You've said over and over again how dangerous this job of yours was and the enemies you've made."

He shook his head and pushed his thumb over her lips. "Yes, dangerous. But I wasn't a spy. Marcus and I, our circles overlapped from time to time, and I assumed that was why God hadn't put someone in my life. But other than Rashid, no one would know my name or be interested in coming after me. I've been out for almost a decade. If they wanted me, they would've come by now."

Tracing from her lips to her jaw, he sighed. "I've never thought about a family, but then again, this is all new territory. I won't say no to the idea if that's what you're worried about."

"So, all this old talk isn't going to change things?"

He chuckled. "I don't feel old with you. Nothing I do feels old with you. I just want you."

Her red lips turned up, and she leaned in, kissing him passionately before he could catch up. Pushing into a hug, she whispered into his ear,

"I guess we'll have to go ring shopping then."

He chuckled and eased her back, standing and pulling the ring from his pocket before he knelt. Her eyes widened and her jaw dropped.

"You think I didn't know exactly what you would like?" He took her hand and slid the ring on her finger. Gazing up into her tear-filled eyes, he smiled. "I love you. I have since the day I met you, and it grows deeper every day. I know I'll love you more tomorrow than I do right now, but it's hard to understand or believe. God led me to you, Olivia. I want you. Will you marry me?"

She managed a breathless "yes" as she pulled him up, grabbing his neck and holding on tight.

Overwhelming happiness washed over him. Love wasn't something he'd had in his life, not since losing his mother. And now, God had given him more than he could imagine.

Holding her tight, he fell over the back of the couch, landing with her on his chest and rolling her to the side as that wonderful laughter of hers filled the air. Kissing her forehead, he closed his eyes as she pressed up against him, holding on.

"Thank you, God," he murmured as he breathed her in, knowing this happiness was what God had planned all along.

ABOUT THE AUTHOR

As a child in northwest Arkansas, Cindy accompanied her father to visit a lot of men and women in nursing homes or their own homes, to offer company and to listen to stories of the good ole days. Most were former military, several having survived World War II, Korea and various other operations.

Her father, both grandfathers and uncles were all former military, so as she grew up, she was inundated with stories of heroes, chaos and the burden of war.

Having listened to stories her whole life, it was easy to put pen to paper and begin her own journey of storytelling. As God led her through grace and mercy in her own life, it was only natural to put it all down on paper and include the hero types she'd heard so much about growing up.

Publishing has been a journey God presented in her current hometown and there's been more and more support from family, friends and local businesses. Her hope is that these stories of God's grace, mercy and love will answer questions and lead others to learn more about Jesus Christ.

ALSO BY CINDY BONDS

Tactical Response Team series:

Fighter

Book One of the Tactical Response Team (TRT)

Bexley Bowers has lost everything during her 30 years . Struggling to find her path, she's targeted and kidnapped by a crazed terrorist.

Evan Mitchell retired from the Navy only to find himself back at work, clinging to his job with the Tactical Response Team. He meets Bexley while on assignment, and a strange tug on his emotions leaves him scrambling. Bexley is too stubborn and too beautiful. He'll never be able to get her out of his mind—especially now that he's her protection.

When Bexley finds herself in trouble, can Evan's team arrive in time?

Fighting the clock and their pride, Evan and Bexley must decide which is more important—their egos or their future.

Get your copy here:

https://scrivenings.link/fighter

Protector

Book Two of the Tactical Response Team (TRT)

Danica Freeman has put her past firmly behind her. She's found happiness and a place to belong within the TRT. But as her new family comes under attack, the chain of events makes her wonder if this is less about the team and something more personal.

Haiden Blake overcame his tragic childhood and found himself in the Army. Now a retired sniper, he uses his skills to protect and defend on American soil. He's found a family in the TRT, but something more with Danica. She's his close friend, as close as he can allow her to become.

Danica and Haiden leave sparks to burn, unwilling to risk it all to move forward to something more. But another attack puts Danica in danger, and Haiden is unable to protect her. At the risk of losing Danica forever, Haiden takes a leap of faith, praying God will catch them both.

Get your copy here:

https://scrivenings.link/protector

Survivor

Book Three of the Tactical Response Team (TRT)

As the Tactical Response Team reels from past attacks, Jeff Powers is determined to figure out who wants them gone. But on the job, he becomes distracted by a beautiful doctor dealing with a stalker.

While helping Dr. Shelby During, Jeff falls deeper and deeper into a strange plot that puts both in grave danger.

Get your copy here:

https://scrivenings.link/survivor

Stand-alone Novels:

***Remains* by Cindy Bonds**

Detective Greer Bennett is not happy the feds are crashing her crime scene. But her instincts are telling her there's more to the story than some whitewashed bones sticking up from an unmarked grave.

Now that Homeland Agent Gage Sullivan has found his sister's remains, he can prosecute the man responsible. But he'll have to find a way to play nice with the detective in charge of the case. And she's not eager to engage.

As they investigate, the body count rises and the clues aren't giving them the answers they need. If they are to survive, the trust Greer is so unwilling to relent will have to come, or the killer will add two more victims to his count—Greer and Gage.

Get your copy here:

https://scrivenings.link/remains

Rainstorm

Laurel Ashburn has a scarred past, filled with corruption and pain. After an injury overseas sends her home, she moves back in with her foster mother and to a town that hates her. Being home puts her on a path to find a missing friend. But when she's attacked over and over, who will be willing to help?

Detective Dev Hollister traded in the big city for a slower pace and less crime in rural Arkansas. After rescuing Laurel from an attempted kidnapping, he finds himself intrigued with this headstrong and stubborn woman.

While Dev's job is to protect Laurel, he wants much more than to solve the case. He wants to give her a new life and reason to stay.

Laurel must push beyond her dark past to trust Dev with her life. But after losing so much, can Laurel survive one more storm?

Get your copy here:

https://scrivenings.link/rainstorm

Hostage

Her confidence shot, Agent Macy Packer desperately wants to go back to her regular life, before she was taken hostage. To forget the pain, the fear and forget the man that helped her through all of it, then disappeared.

Kane Bledsoe is finally healed, his scars serving as a reminder of his time in captivity. But all he can think about is the blue-eyed woman that saved him. She had saved them all and left him with a burning hope.

A chance meeting and an attack prove Macy is still in danger.

Kane pushes himself into the investigation, doing what he can to provide protection.

The enemy is clear—he wants Macy.

Kane will have to decide just how far he's willing to go to protect her. Can he sacrifice himself when the time comes?

Get your copy here:

https://scrivenings.link/hostage

Stay up-to-date on your favorite books and authors with our free e-newsletters.

ScriveningsPress.com

www.ingramcontent.com/pod-product-compliance
Lightning Source LLC
Chambersburg PA
CBHW070621100726
47907CB00007B/1820